*Every darned woman in the world was attracted to Tanner.*

And Bailey wasn't any different, except that she had dreams and visions, and they didn't include settling down with a man.

At least, not yet. She was only twenty-five. Not that Tanner would want anything permanent with her, anyway. Since he and his ex had split up years ago, he hadn't dated anybody for longer than a month. And those he had dated didn't come from West Virginia. They were New York socialites or the daughters of influential men or executive directors of charities who donated back their salaries because they didn't need them.

Bailey was just about certain that Tanner wouldn't consider dating the town beautician.

In the end she wouldn't be good enough.

And plus, there were the rumors....

Dear Reader,

*Get Caught Reading*. It sounds slightly scandalous, romantic and definitely exciting! I love to get lost in a book, and this month we're joining the campaign to encourage reading everywhere. Share your favorite books with your partner, your child, your friends. And be sure to get caught reading yourself!

The popular ROYALLY WED series continues with Valerie Parv's *Code Name: Prince*. King Michael is still missing—but there's a plan to rescue him! In *Quinn's Complete Seduction* Sandra Steffen returns to BACHELOR GULCH, where Crystal finally finds what she's been searching for— and more....

*Chance's Joy* launches Patricia Thayer's exciting new miniseries, THE TEXAS BROTHERHOOD. In the first story, Chance Randell wants to buy his lovely neighbor's land, but hadn't bargained for a wife and baby! In *McKinley's Miracle*, talented Mary Kate Holder debuts with the story of a rugged Australian rancher who meets his match.

Susan Meier is sure to please with *Marrying Money*, in which a small-town beautician makes a rich man rethink his reasons for refusing love. And Myrna Mackenzie gives us *The Billionaire Is Back,* in which a wealthy playboy fights a strong attraction to his pregnant, single cook!

Come back next month for the triumphant conclusion to ROYALLY WED and more wonderful stories by Patricia Thayer and Myrna Mackenzie. Silhouette Romance always gives you stories that will touch your emotions and carry you away....

Be sure to *Get Caught Reading!*

*Mary-Theresa Hussey*

Mary-Theresa Hussey
Senior Editor

Please address questions and book requests to:
Silhouette Reader Service
U.S.: 3010 Walden Ave., P.O. Box 1325, Buffalo, NY 14269
Canadian: P.O. Box 609, Fort Erie, Ont. L2A 5X3

# Marrying Money

## SUSAN MEIER

SILHOUETTE *Romance*

Published by Silhouette Books

America's Publisher of Contemporary Romance

I would like to dedicate this book
to Karen Taylor Richman for all her help over the years.

 SILHOUETTE BOOKS

ISBN 0-373-19519-2

MARRYING MONEY

Copyright © 2001 by Linda Susan Meier

Visit Silhouette at www.eHarlequin.com

Printed in U.S.A.

**Books by Susan Meier**

Silhouette Romance

*Stand-in Mom* #1022
*Temporarily Hers* #1109
*Wife in Training* #1184
*Merry Christmas, Daddy* #1192
*In Care of the Sheriff* #1283
*Guess What? We're Married!* #1338
*Husband from 9 to 5* #1354
*The Rancher and the Heiress* #1374
†*The Baby Bequest* #1420
†*Bringing up Babies* #1427
†*Oh, Babies!* #1433
*His Expectant Neighbor* #1468
*Hunter's Vow* #1487
*Cinderella and the CEO* #1498
*Marrying Money* #1519

*Texas Family Ties
†Brewster Baby Boom

Silhouette Desire

*Take the Risk* #567

# SUSAN MEIER

has written category romances for Silhouette Romance and Silhouette Desire. A full-time writer, Susan has also been an employee of a major defense contractor, a columnist for a small newspaper and a division manager of a charitable organization. But her greatest joy in her life has always been her children, who constantly surprise and amaze her. Married for over twenty years to her wonderful, understanding and gorgeous husband, Michael, Susan cherishes her role as a mother, wife, sister and friend, believing them to be life's real treasures. She not only cherishes those roles as gifts, she tries to convey the beauty and importance of loving relationships in her books.

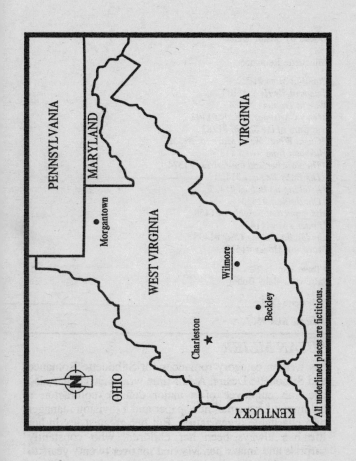

PENNSYLVANIA

MARYLAND

VIRGINIA

OHIO

WEST VIRGINIA

KENTUCKY

Morgantown

Charleston

Wilmore

Beckley

N

All underlined places are fictitious.

# Chapter One

"I can't believe I'm doing this," Tanner McConnell mumbled as he drove his Mercedes into a parking space in the lot of the newly remodeled church hall in Wilmore, West Virginia.

"What was that, dear?"

Recognizing he'd grumbled loud enough for his mother to hear, Tanner cleared his throat, pretending his unintentional comment had been a cough. "Nothing, Mother. Just a little frog in my throat, that's all."

He got out of the car and rounded the hood. Because it was a warm June evening, and fifteen minutes remained before dinner would be served, people gathered in small conversation groups around the huge oaks and flower beds that surrounded the gray block building. Most of the men yanked at their collars, uncomfortable in their suit jackets, white shirts and ties, while their wives virtually glowed in semiformal wear and fancy upswept hairdos.

As Tanner walked around the front of the car to the

passenger side, his father exited the back seat of the Mercedes and opened the car door for Tanner's mother.

"Don't buy that cough story," Jim McConnell said. "What Tanner mumbled was that he can't believe we talked him into coming to this celebration dinner." He offered a hand to his wife to assist her from her seat. "Thinks he's too good for us now," he added in a stage whisper, then winked.

Tanner was a replica of his green-eyed, sandy-haired father, who remained as muscled and fit as he had been in his youth when he'd taught Tanner to play football. Jim always claimed Tanner's mother, Doris, was still as beautiful as the day he met her. Looking at her, dressed in the coral-colored cocktail suit she had purchased on a trip to New York City with Tanner a few months before, her dark auburn hair tucked into a neat chignon and just the right amount of makeup accenting her round brown eyes, Tanner believed it. He had always been proud of his parents and proud of his life. He simply didn't want to live it in Wilmore.

"You know that's not it," Tanner replied. "It's just that I really don't care to see Emmalee, that's all."

"I don't know why. Your divorce was final years ago," Doris said, adjusting her son's paisley tie. "Emmalee's married to the mayor now. She moved on years ago."

"And so did I," Tanner said. Though everyone else wore a standard-fare black or navy suit, Tanner didn't feel out of place in the expensive cocoa-brown suit and ivory shirt he'd had specially made for him, because he knew people in this town expected him to look the part of who he was. "In case either of you has forgotten, I just sold my trucking company for a small fortune. I've *more* than moved on. I'm moving on *again*."

"We know, dear," his mother said, using her calm, conciliatory voice. "You're a rich, successful ex-college football star who blew out his knee his first game in the pros and used his compensation money to start a trucking company that you sold for millions. We haven't forgotten any of that." She paused long enough to smile at her son. "But you're also not married."

"And we don't have grandbabies," Jim put in, peeking around Doris as the trio began to walk across the parking lot to the crowded, noisy church hall.

"Oh," Tanner said, sighing with understanding. "So that's what this is all about." He looked over at the town celebration with new eyes. "You think I'll find a wife tonight."

"No better place to find a good woman than your hometown," Jim said.

"There are at least fifteen lovely young women who are unattached and who would make you a fabulous wife," Doris added as if spouse shopping were an everyday occurrence and Tanner shouldn't be insulted that his parents had brought him to their version of a matrimony mall.

Over his mother's head, Tanner scowled at his father.

"Hey, don't make faces at me. Your mother and I are in this together," Jim said.

Passing the small groups clustered in front of the entry, Tanner and his parents issued greetings and exchanged pleasantries but didn't actually stop to talk. They walked to the admission window immediately inside the open door of the church hall. A petite blonde was collecting tickets.

Wearing an ink-blue sequined tank dress with a filmy, frilly ruffle at the hemline about five inches above her knees, and earrings and a necklace that seemed to be the

exact hue of her dress, she looked as though she should
be on television or on a magazine cover, not welcoming
patrons to a dinner dance in a tiny town in the Appala-
chian Mountains.

"Hello, Mr. McConnell, Mrs. McConnell..." She
paused and looked at Tanner. "Tanner," she added
softly.

Her voice reminded him of a lullaby. Wistful, light,
airy and full of warmth. Her eyes were the color of wild
violets. Her thick yellow hair was piled on her head in
some sort of fancy hairdo that made him think of a Greek
goddess. Strands slipped and curled from the main mass,
and a long strip hung from the back like a silken water-
fall. Spellbound, he stared at her.

"You remember Bailey Stephenson," his mother said.
"She owns the beauty shop."

Tanner smiled. Of course...who else would have hair
that looked like a work of art? "I'm sorry, I don't remember you," he said, then extended his hand, suddenly
awfully darned glad his parents had insisted he attend this
celebration of the town's triumphant renewal after the
unexpectedly severe spring flooding.

She took Tanner's hand, her smooth, thin palm sliding
along the calluses of his much bigger, much stronger
palm, and Tanner could swear his heart stopped. She had
skin like warm velvet and small, delicate, feminine bones
that reminded him that he was not only considerably
larger than she was, but also that he was a man and she
was a woman.

Heat tingled through him. Mesmerized, confused, he
gazed into her eyes, and he couldn't seem to let go of
her hand. With women throwing themselves at his feet
at every turn, some because of his money, some because
of his looks, it had been a long, long time since Tanner

had spontaneously reacted to a woman. Not only did he like the feeling, but he wanted it to go on forever.

"I didn't think you would remember me," Bailey said, smiling at him, not like a woman who was flirting, but like a woman who saw him as an equal, as a person, not a personality.

Full-fledged attraction shot through him. There was no doubt about it. He liked this woman—instantly, instinctively liked this woman. Not merely because she was beautiful but because he knew that if she were attracted to him it would be for reasons other than superficial ones.

"I'm a little younger than you are," she added. "When you left town I was probably only starting high school."

Before Tanner had a chance to do the math on that and fret over the fact that she might be too young for him, his father muttered an oath.

"Ah, damn," Jim said, as he patted his suit jacket pocket. "I forgot the tickets."

"That's okay," the pretty beautician said, smiling at his parents. "Your names are on the list. The tickets are only a formality."

"Are you sure?" Doris asked.

"Of course I'm sure. I chaired the committee, remember?" Bailey said with a laugh. "But, if you would like to give the committee a good-faith gesture, your son could—"

"I'll do whatever you want," Tanner cut in with a grin, happy to seize any chance to get close to and stay close to this woman.

"Well, don't speak too soon." Bailey bit back a smile. "I was about to volunteer you for the revitalization committee."

Tanner's grin faded. "What?"

"The members of the restoration committee, which managed the actual flood cleanup, decided we need a revitalization committee because there are so many things this town needs that one committee couldn't handle it all."

He stared at her.

She began ticking off items on her fingers. "We need a park for the kids. We could use some bike trails. A community college would be the best thing that could happen for our young people. And we need a senior center. There are grants and Federal money available for most of that, but we need people dedicated to going after them."

"I—" Tanner began.

"Tanner can't serve on a committee," his mother interrupted, speaking for him as if he weren't standing right beside her. "I think he would be perfect—all that business experience of his could help the town enormously— but the entire time he was building his business, he dreamed of retiring in Florida. Buying a boat. Taking people on chartered fishing tours to make pocket change while he played. He's not interested."

"Too bad," Bailey said casually. "Well, you three have a good time tonight," she added, turning her attention to the incoming group behind them.

Tanner *didn't* want to serve on the committee, but he should have had the opportunity to make up his own mind. "Thank you very much, Mom. The least I could have done was hear Bailey out about the responsibilities of serving on the committee."

That stopped him. Actually, hearing her out *was* the least he could do to get another five, ten or maybe even twenty minutes with her. He certainly wasn't going to let the first woman who had piqued his interest in ten years get away without a conversation.

Bailey Stephenson watched Tanner walk into the main room of the church hall, which was decorated in a sea of red, white and blue crepe paper, the rows of long narrow tables covered with white plastic cloths and sporting fat red candles and miniature flags as centerpieces. She bit her lower lip as she collected the tickets of the Franklin family. It had been everything she could do to suppress a shiver when Tanner McConnell had taken her hand, but the truth was that every darned woman in the world was attracted to him. She wasn't any different from anybody else, except that she had goals and visions, and they didn't include settling down with a man.

At least not yet. She was only twenty-five. Too young to be thinking about anything permanent...not that she thought Tanner McConnell would want something permanent with her. Since he and Emmalee split up all those years ago, he hadn't dated anybody for more than a month. And those he had dated didn't come from West Virginia. They were New York socialites. He didn't even date models and actresses. His taste ran to daughters of influential men. Or executive directors of charities who donated back their salaries because they didn't need them. Or patrons of the ballet and symphony. Bailey was just about certain that Tanner wouldn't consider the town beautician to be a member of that category. In the end she wouldn't be good enough, just like Emmalee hadn't been good enough to move with him when he left Wilmore to start his new life.

At least that was the rumor.

Besides, she didn't care about Emma and Tanner and their ugly divorce. She had work to do. With her business degree languishing away while she focused on creating great hairdos to build the customer base of her beauty shop, she needed a way to keep sharp the skills she'd learned in college. And fate had given her the perfect opportunity. When she and the members of the flood recovery committee had realized how many things their town lacked and how easy it would be to get them if a few people dedicated time to going after the money, she knew this was the way to make sure she didn't get rusty. And she also knew she had more than enough to keep her occupied. There was no room for a man in her life.

As she joined the group inside, she caught Tanner staring at her. When she caught Tanner staring at her all through dinner, she decided she had confused him by not falling at his feet...which was understandable since everybody else did. When he tried to mingle in her direction before the band started, she adroitly sidestepped all his attempts. But when he cornered her just as the band played its first romantic song, a lovely lilting waltz, Bailey knew there was no dodging the inevitable.

"Dance?" he asked, extending his hand to her and giving her the perfect, glorious smile that melted most women.

Right on cue, Bailey felt her knees weaken. His green eyes sparkled with sincerity. His tanned skin brought out the best in his sandy-brown hair, which was streaked with blond from the sun. He had a straight nose and even straighter teeth. It almost seemed that when he was created, the universe set out to combine the best of everything, and it had definitely succeeded.

When she didn't answer him, he stepped a little closer, opened his hand a little wider. "It's only a dance," he coaxed, but Bailey didn't think so. When she looked into the depths of his eyes, instincts she didn't know she possessed surged to the forefront. She could fall madly in love with him. Quickly. Easily. Any woman could. And he would hurt her. She wasn't any more sophisticated than Emmalee had been, so undoubtedly he would drop her after a date or two. Since she wasn't the kind for a casual fling or temporary relationship, she was just a tad too naive for the likes of Tanner McConnell.

Still staring into his eyes, she swallowed, then said, "I don't think so. I should go into the kitchen to make sure the cleanup committee isn't having any trouble."

She turned to go, but Tanner caught her hand and spun her around again. "It's not a good idea to micromanage."

"What?"

"It's never a good idea to micromanage," he said, easily manipulating her onto the dance floor by preoccupying her with the explanation of what he had said. "Because you're the committee head," he added, his arm casually, smoothly sliding across the small of her back, "you're everybody's boss. If you keep going back to check on them, people will think you don't trust them."

"They won't think I care about them and I'm trying to keep up my end of the work?" she asked, while inside her heart tripped out a frantic rhythm, and awareness of him hummed through her. Tall and masculine, picture-perfect gorgeous, with a smile that forced her to smile in response, Tanner McConnell incited feelings and sensations in her that were probably illegal in conservative states.

Tanner laughed, effortlessly guiding her around the dance floor in a waltz. "No. They'll think you're robbing them of an opportunity to please you, to impress you."

She tilted her head in question. He was such a handsome man that people forgot he was also ultrasuccessful.

Someday Bailey wanted to be ultrasuccessful, too. If fate was giving her nudges in his direction, maybe it wasn't for romance, but to get his guidance. "Is that how you ran your business?"

He nodded. "Put enough faith in people, show them you believe they can succeed, and they will do anything you ask."

She smiled. "Really?"

"Really."

"That is so interesting, because I just hired a new stylist who is very talented, but when it comes to the crunch hairdos, she just sort of freaks out on me."

"Crunch hairdos?"

"The big deals," Bailey explained, catching his gaze. "You know, wedding parties, upsweeps for the prom, the important hairdos."

"Oh, those are your critical success factors for your business," he said, understanding.

"Precisely. Those are the things that make or break you. Owning the beauty shop is like being the florist. If a bride likes the flowers you do for her wedding, she'll get her mother's day bouquets from you. If a girl likes the way you do her hair for the prom, you're a shoo-in to do her wedding."

Tanner nodded approvingly, like a man who was not only listening, but also comprehending, but Bailey suddenly felt incredibly stupid. She was dancing with the most attractive man in the world and though she knew talking about business was the best way to keep herself out of trouble, talking about upsweeps for the prom might be carrying things too far.

She licked her lips, trying to think of something to say, but when she caught his gaze again the words died on her tongue. As he swept her around the floor, with her feet feeling as if they were barely touching the ground, the ruffle of her dress flowing around her, and the room spinning by, she felt like a princess. Mesmerized by his beautiful green eyes, she couldn't help but wish this dance, this moment, could go on forever. She felt his hand tighten at her waist, watched his lips as they bowed upward into a broad smile, and her stomach sank to the floor. She had never wanted anything so much in her entire life, in spite of the fact that she knew it was dead wrong and that she wasn't going to get it.

She almost willed the band to play an extra chorus and when they did she used that unexpected gift of two more minutes to memorize his scent, the look in his eyes, the way his hand felt on the small of her back. She remembered every tingle resonating through her, every pinpoint of awareness inspired by his touch, every good and happy thought that raced through her brain. Because when the song was over and they broke apart to applaud she knew she would do what she had to do.

She faced him, smiled and politely said, "Thank you for the dance," then ran like the wind into the kitchen.

A quick glance around the stainless steel and Formica room told her everything had been wiped down, washed or returned to its proper position. She faced Ricky Avery, ready to ask him if certain tasks had been done, but remembering the business advice Tanner had given her as he held her in his arms, she smiled and said, "Looks good in here."

Tall, lanky, curly haired Ricky beamed and peered around with self-satisfaction. "You think so?"

"Yeah," she said, patting his shoulder. "You did very, very well. I'm proud of you."

Ricky straightened his shoulders and suddenly looked ten feet tall. "Thanks."

Bailey smiled. "You're welcome," she said, then grabbed the purse she had left with the kitchen staff for safekeeping. "I'll see you around town," she added, and started for the door.

Ricky gave her a puzzled frown. "You're leaving?"

"I've already had enough excitement for one night. Besides, I'm working in the morning."

"But tomorrow's Sunday."

"Somebody's still got to comb out all those up-dos," Bailey quickly countered. "If everybody wraps their hair for bed tonight like I told them, they'll be okay for church in the morning, but after church nobody's going to want to walk around in blue jeans and a T-shirt, looking like Athena."

"But you planned this...and the night's only started," Ricky protested, obviously confused.

Bailey smiled a response, but seeing that Tanner had finally made his way to the kitchen and was about to walk through the door, she said, "I know. See you tomorrow."

She raced out into the dark, empty night. In her haste she was very careful to make sure she didn't lose one of her shoes because then for sure she would have felt like Cinderella leaving the ball. And she wasn't. She was a beautician from Wilmore, West Virginia, trying to build a business, trying to help her town. She was a common, simple, ordinary woman. Not royalty. Not a princess destined to marry a prince.

She climbed into her SUV and shoved the key in the ignition just in time to see Tanner come out of the back door of the church hall. He waved. She yanked her gearshift into drive and drove off. Content with one dance. One very happy memory.

# Chapter Two

But Tanner wasn't nearly satisfied with a memory. He trudged back into the red, white and blue church hall, his lips pursed, his mind going a million miles a second.

"She dumped you," his father said casually as Tanner pulled out a folding chair and sat beside his mother.

Tanner loosened his tie and grimaced. "She went home. Ricky Avery said she said something about having to comb out up-dos in the morning."

"If she said she does, she does," Tanner's mother confirmed, then popped an olive in her mouth. "Not everybody's retired like you are."

"No kidding," Tanner said.

"In fact, she just bought her beauty shop from Flora Mae Houser. Flora Mae had it for the past thirty years. You probably don't remember her, but she was the woman who—"

Tanner scowled at his mother.

"Sorry, dear," she said, then smiled. "I keep forgetting my two men hate it when I switch topics without warning. We can go back to talking about how Bailey doesn't want to have anything to do with you."

"If she hadn't just run like her shoes were on fire, I would have sworn you set this up for me to meet her," Tanner grumbled. There wasn't another woman in the room who came close to Bailey. Nobody else he cared to even talk to, let alone dance with. And his parents would have known he'd like her from the first hello.

"Not me," Jim McConnell said.

"Not me, either," Doris seconded. "Nobody sets anything up for a woman like Bailey. Besides, look around you. There are plenty of fish in this proverbial sea. Just go ask somebody to dance."

"I'm out of the mood," Tanner said, rising from his seat. "I think I'll go home, too."

Doris smiled. "You can't go home. You drove us, remember?"

He sighed. Now he knew for sure his parents hadn't set him up with Bailey. If they had, they wouldn't have ridden with him in his car. They would have given him access to drive Bailey home. Or to follow her when she ran, since his mother probably knew Bailey would leave early because of work. He hadn't been set up. His parents didn't want him married to Bailey Stephenson. They simply wanted him married.

Tanner's mother waved her hand in the direction of the crowd. "Go ask somebody to dance. Your good mood will come back."

Tanner didn't bother to argue that he hadn't been in a good mood about this dinner dance until he met Bailey. He didn't want to mention it to his parents, because then he would have to explain it to himself. And if he started explaining it to himself he would have to use words like *intrigued, fascinated,* maybe even *smitten.* Which was ridiculous. He'd hardly said two words to the woman. He couldn't be interested in someone he didn't know beyond eye color and occupation. Besides, she obviously didn't want to have anything to do with him. He couldn't be *smitten* with someone who didn't even like him. It wasn't normal.

It was for that very reason that Tanner rousted himself from his seat and did ask a few of the eligible women to dance. But though lovely, intelligent and fun, none of them seemed to intrigue him the way Bailey had. He didn't know what it was about her that drew him, but something did. And it was something more than the fact that she was a challenge. She fit in his arms. She smelled wonderful. And he saw those darned violet eyes of hers the minute he closed his eyes that night in bed.

In church the next morning, Tanner decided he was just tired, and overwhelmed from selling his business on the spur of the moment and drastically changing his life. There would be plenty of women in Florida, maybe even a woman who knew more about operating a charter boat business than he did. He didn't need Bailey Stephenson. Hell, he wasn't even sure he *wanted* Bailey Stephenson. Half of what he thought he felt might have been his imagination. He was a happy guy with a great life and a future most people would fight for. He had everything he wanted and needed.

Unfortunately, just as he got himself comfortable with that thought, Mayor Thorpe and his wife Emmalee marched down the center aisle with their three perfectly behaved, well-dressed children. Tanner's heart sank. The family, the life Emmalee had now was exactly what they'd envisioned having together. Except if she had stayed married to Tanner, Emma would have had a bigger house and more security. Yet, she'd dumped him. Tanner wasn't such a simpleton that he thought money meant more than love, but she *had* loved him. He had loved her. They'd been crazy about each other. But here she was, walking down the center aisle of the church with another man's children.

Even after ten years it still hurt. Not that he wasn't over her. He was. He knew that the man he'd become couldn't live the life she had here in Wilmore. He needed more. He needed different things. And he usually got them, because, when the need arose, he could be ruthless.

Single-minded, self-centered and ruthless.

Emmalee was, in fact, the person who had told him that. She had told him to move on because his big dreams had changed him and he didn't fit in this town anymore. She was tired of pretending that he was great and wonderful to grace them with his presence a few times a month, faking that he belonged here when he didn't. He belonged anywhere but quiet, mellow Wilmore. She was even the one who suggested that he try living somewhere like New York where aggressiveness was an art, not a transgression.

So he did move and he discovered she was right. He did fit better in a bigger city. But just because she had hit the nail on the head, that didn't mean it hadn't hurt like hell to lose his wife and his hometown all in one quick swoop.

Which was exactly why he knew he had to stay away from Bailey Stephenson and every other woman in this town. He didn't belong here. Even a woman who had adored him had known it and sent him packing. He was only here now to supervise the repair of the flood damage to his parents' property, and to say goodbye to some old friends before he moved a thousand miles away, because when the month was out, he was off to Florida. And he wasn't coming back. Not even for sporadic visits. The plan was that his parents would visit *him*, not vice versa. He would never return to West Virginia. So there was no sense making any more ties.

He felt comfortable with that assessment and even took a minute to objectively appreciate how adorable Emmalee's kids were and to recognize that Artie Thorpe was definitely more suited to being Emma's husband than Tanner had been. And he happily realized he could probably hold a pleasant conversation with them after the service.

And then Bailey walked in.

Unlike the other women who still sported sagging upsweeps from the night before, Bailey's blond hair hung straight and silky to the middle of her back. Wearing a simple floral sheath that accented her curves and showed off her long, shapely legs, Bailey Stephenson was everything he remembered from the night before, and every feeling, every sensation he had while dancing with her came flooding back.

Tanner completely forgot about Artie and Emma Thorpe. He forgot he didn't belong in this town. He forgot that half the congregation was undoubtedly watching him. All he could do was stare at Bailey and remember the fluttering in his stomach when he looked at her, when he danced with her.

She turned to walk into the pew she had chosen and caught sight of Tanner and his parents. Tanner's mother gave Bailey the subtle, fingers-only wave women used for a greeting when they were trying to be discreet, and Bailey returned the smile and the wave, her gaze straying to Tanner.

He almost sighed with relief, because from the look in

her eyes it was obvious she found him attractive, too. But when it appeared hard for her to pull her gaze away from his, the fluttering in his stomach flared again. By the time she sat down and the service started, Tanner not only forgot all about the pain of the past, he had shifted back into his normal way of looking at things. His rule of thumb was to make the best of the life he had, not pine for the one he'd lost. And right now he had a sixth sense that fate was handing him the chance to spend some time with an absolutely stunning, unpretentious woman. He almost grinned. Life was incredibly good to him.

He actually found himself timing the sermon with growing irritation. Reverend Daniels seemed to be in a particularly talkative mood. With every five-minute segment that ticked off on Tanner's watch, his squirming grew more evident. But because Bailey's squirming grew more evident, too, he was absolutely positive they would literally run into each other's arms at the end of the service. However, when the good pastor finally let them go, Bailey exploded from the church and scrambled to her car…not to him.

Standing on the church steps, too far away to even hope to catch her, Tanner had to forcefully stop himself from cursing out loud.

"Hey, Tanner."

Tanner turned to see Artie and Emma and three little blond munchkins huddled around them, looking as if they were velcroed to their parents' knees. With thoughts of Bailey still clouding his brain, he automatically smiled his public-relations smile and extended his hand to Artie. "Hi, Artie," he said, shaking his hand. "Emma," he added, nodding to his ex-wife. "Who are these guys?"

"I'm Sam," the first child said, then he sniffed.

"Oh, darn," Emma said, sounding exasperated. "We forgot his allergy medicine this morning."

Sam sniffed more loudly. "That's okay."

"No, it's not, Samuel Eugene Thorpe," Emma said. A tall beauty, with red hair and porcelain skin, Emma made a pretty picture as a mother. "You might not like to take those pills, but you need them!" She faced Tanner again. "I'm sorry, Tanner, but we've got to go."

"Hey, never let it be said that I stood in the way of proper child care."

"How long are you in town?" she asked, studying him cautiously.

Tanner's gaze strolled in the direction Bailey's SUV had taken and then he pulled it back to his ex-wife. "I don't know."

"Well," Emma said carefully, glancing at her husband who was talking to Dave Banister, one of the town's two councilmen. "I think you and I need to talk. There's some stuff—"

"After ten years," Tanner interrupted. "I doubt it, Emma."

He hadn't intended to be so cool or so cruel, but those darned memories crept up on him when he didn't want them to. Ten years ago she had her say and she had succinctly told him what a terrible husband he was. And he agreed. As a husband, he was a washout. But right now he didn't need to be reminded that the prettiest girl from his high school class had dumped him. Especially not when the pretty beautician who currently intrigued him—the woman he instinctively knew was the one he was supposed to be spending time with—wouldn't give him that time, probably because she'd heard the rumors about his divorce. Again this confirmed what Emma had said the day she asked him to leave: in New York, he could do absolutely anything he wanted. In West Virginia his past haunted him. After he got to Florida, he would send Emma flowers with an apology to make up for his rudeness, but right now he just wanted to go home.

Luckily, his parents were starving and had done a lot of socializing last night so they'd all headed back to the house. Feeling spurned by Bailey without a real chance to explain himself or his intentions, Tanner wasn't surprised that he devised a plan to see her while his mother was putting the finishing touches on lunch. And it also didn't surprise him when he left the house with a mumbled apology before the food was served. Because he really wasn't hungry. He felt like a man with a mission. Not that he was going to force Bailey to go out with him or even to pay attention to him. He had never had to use manipulation or coercion with a woman. And he was sure that, given an opportunity to see that he wasn't a bad guy—he was just a sort of transient guy—Bailey wouldn't have to be forced, either.

After rushing to her apartment to change into jeans and a T-shirt, and racing to her parents' house to have a quick lunch with her family, Bailey hurried to her shop. But when she arrived it wasn't to discover a line of impatient, flat-haired women awaiting her. Bailey only found Tanner McConnell on the top step leading to her salon door. He was handsome enough that even dressed in simple jeans and a plain white polo shirt, with his short sandy-brown hair ruffled by the June breeze and his green eyes clear and direct, watching her every move as she exited her SUV, the man could stop women's hearts. But not hers. She had already had this conversation with herself.

She frowned. "What are you doing here?"

"I want you to comb out my up-do."

He said it so sincerely that Bailey giggled. "You don't have an up-do. In fact, you could never get an up-do. Your hair is too short."

"You want to restyle it?" he asked hopefully.

She shook her head. "No. It's fine the way it is...great actually."

He smiled. "Really? You like it? I mean, that's your professional opinion?"

She nodded. "Yeah. Whoever styled your hair knew exactly what he was doing."

"Roberto will be relieved I'm sure."

"Good. Go call him now to tell him, because I have work to do."

"You're blowing me off again."

Fumbling with her keys, she managed the dual purpose of avoiding his eyes and unlocking her shop. "No, I'm not."

"Good, then trim my hair. Leave the style just like Roberto has it, but take off that annoying fraction of an inch or so that keeps getting in my way."

Leading him into the spotlessly clean shop, she said, "You're not serious."

"Is this a hair salon?" he asked, looking around at the four black stylists chairs, low-bowled chrome sinks and white-hooded dryers.

She nodded.

"Are you open for business?"

This time Bailey sighed. She knew she had no choice but to do what he wanted. Because if she told him she wasn't open and one of her regulars came by to get rid of her day-old curls from the celebration, Bailey wouldn't be able to take her in. At this point, with a huge business loan and customers not quite sure if they wanted to be loyal to the shop or try their luck somewhere else, Bailey couldn't afford to offend anyone.

"I'm open."

"Okay, then. I want my hair trimmed."

She directed Tanner to sit on her salon chair, and pulled out the big black cape she used to cover the clothes of customers. She draped it over his white polo shirt and jeans. "I see you went home and changed after church, like I did."

"Is that where you went?" he asked casually, but from the looks he had given her all through the service Bailey knew he had been planning to chat with her and undoubtedly she irritated him by speeding off.

"To change and to have lunch with my family," she explained, occupied now with selecting scissors.

"That's nice. You must be close to your family," he said. He sounded truly interested, but Bailey didn't think it was prudent to get into a personal discussion with him. No sense in encouraging him when they didn't have a future together. He wasn't staying in Wilmore, and even if by some miracle he fell madly in love with her, she was tied to the town by a big loan. He could not carry her off on his white horse. No one could. She was stuck here.

She brushed her fingers through the back of his already-short hair and was surprised by how silky it was. "Your hair doesn't really need to be trimmed, you know."

"Sure it does," he insisted.

"Okay," she said, combing her nails through the short, satiny locks again. She had cut enough hair in her lifetime that she thought she had felt all possible combinations of textures and naps, but there was something unsettlingly different about Tanner's hair. It tingled against her fingertips and palm, as if it were alive.

She cleared her throat. "I'm only taking off about an eighth of an inch."

"That's good. That's about how much I figure has been getting in the way when I blow dry."

The very absurdity of that statement made her laugh again. "Stop that," she said, but she sounded like a silly schoolgirl flirting with the star athlete.

"Why? Don't you like to laugh?"

"I love to laugh, but if you're smart you won't want the person who has scissors to your head to get a case of the giggles. I could ruin your hair."

"It would grow back."

She drew in a resigned breath. "Do you always have an answer for everything?"

"Yes," he said, quickly, concisely. He was so serious about it that he caught her wrist to prevent her scissors from reaching his hair, and he turned on the chair to face her. "Yes, I have an answer for everything, so if you would just tell me why you keep avoiding me I could probably resolve the issue in your mind and we could have a good time while I'm here in Wilmore."

"Oh, I see," she said. She wiggled her wrist from his grasp, set her scissors on the counter and untied the smock he wore to protect his clothes from the hair she would have cut, if she had cut any. "That's what this is all about. You don't like rejection."

"I take rejection just fine. I not only started a new business, I ran it for eight years. I know all about rejection. And this has nothing to do with rejection. *I like you.*"

"We haven't even had a twenty-minute conversation," Bailey said, leaning against her counter and crossing her arms on her chest. "How can you say you like me? You don't even know me."

"And you don't know me enough to keep blowing me off like this," Tanner countered with a smile. "So have dinner with me tonight. We'll get to know each other and then we can make an informed decision."

Bailey shook her head. "I don't think so."

"Why not?" Tanner asked, sounding totally confused.

She would have told him there was no future for them and, therefore, no point in their going out, but before the words clearly formed in her brain, her shop door opened.

"Hi, Bailey," Norma Alexander greeted, then she saw Tanner. "Oops! Sorry!" she said, her eyes wide and round with surprise. "I thought you were open for business."

"I am open for business. Tanner was just leaving."

"Actually, Norma," Tanner said, pulling out all his charm and pouring it on poor unsuspecting Norma through his warm, sincere voice, broad smile and earnest eyes. "I could use about another five minutes with Bailey. If you wouldn't mind..."

"She minds!" Bailey said, grabbing Norma's arm to guide her into the shop. "For Pete's sake, Tanner. I'm trying to make a living here."

"Okay, then, you asked for this," Tanner said, his eyes narrowing as if he had calculated this risk and decided to take it. "I want to have dinner with you tonight, and I'm not taking no for an answer."

Norma's eyes lit up and she said, "Oh!" as if she had been witness to an historic event.

Bailey shook her head, refusing him in spite of his declaration that he wouldn't take no for an answer. "No."

"Give me one good reason."

"I have a committee meeting."

"I thought the whole purpose of that dinner dance last night was to celebrate that the flood cleanup was over. You shouldn't be having meetings anymore."

"You forgot the revitalization committee, the one your mother said you couldn't join because you're leaving town."

He sighed. "No, I haven't forgotten."

"We're meeting tonight."

"What kind of committee meets on a Sunday night?" he asked.

Obviously exasperated, he took a few steps in her direction, as if being closer could somehow sway things in his favor. When he got to within a foot of her and her pulse began to scramble, her breathing felt heavy and the blood virtually tingled through her veins, Bailey recognized he was right. Since his nearness endangered her sanity, there was a very real possibility that she would agree to anything he wanted...right before she melted into a puddle at his feet.

Playing with the locket at her neck, she looked him in the eyes and didn't say anything until she had mustered her most firm, most authoritative voice. What came out was more like a squeak, but at least she was still standing.

"The kind with a lot of busy people on it."

Apparently sensing victory because of her shaky voice, he smiled. "Tomorrow night, then?"

"Shop's open Monday nights."

"Tuesday?"

"It's hot wing night at my dad's bar."

"Great. I'll see you there."

"All you'll do is *see* me because I waitress. I won't have time to stop and chat."

"Are you *ever* free?" he asked in exasperation.

Bailey grinned. "Nope."

Glancing from Tanner to Bailey and then back again, Norma laughed. "Tanner McConnell, I think you'd better give up before Bailey ruins your reputation of being a ladies man."

Tanner turned his smile on Norma again. "I wouldn't be placing any money on that bet if I were you."

Norma giggled with happiness, but Bailey felt her heart swell with the frustration of wanting something she couldn't have. She was very tempted to throw caution to the wind and spend some time with him. But all she had to do was glance around at her shop to realize she couldn't afford three months of depression after he left her. She had utility bills, stylists' salaries and a big loan to pay. Depression would stop all that cold.

"Okay, Tanner," she said, then pointed him to her door. "I have work to do. Fun's over."

He smiled. "The fun's only begun Bailey," he said, then pivoted and made the best exit Bailey had ever seen anyone make through Flora Mae's old shop door. Not just because he was smiling and walking tall, but because both Norma and Bailey got a very nice view of his back profile.

Norma sighed with female appreciation.

Bailey sighed, too. "You can say that again."

Happy to have shaken up Bailey the way she continually shook him, Tanner left the salon. But as soon as he stepped out into the Sunday-afternoon sunshine, he realized he didn't have a darned thing to be happy about. He hadn't gotten a date. He really hadn't made any headway. She obviously had her reasons for not wanting to go out with him, but he still didn't know what they were. So far all she had given him were excuses, not reasons.

Though the obvious guess was that she was afraid to get involved with him because of the rumors after his divorce, he had a weird sense that Bailey couldn't be scared off by something like that; she wouldn't blindly believe gossip. She would give him a chance to have his say. So her reasons had to be more practical, more personal, but he still didn't know what the hell they were.

With a sigh he started walking toward his car, but when he stopped to insert the key into the lock, he heard someone calling him.

"Tanner! Tanner McConnell!"

Tanner glanced up and saw Joe Johnson, one of his high school football teammates. "Hey, Joe!" he greeted as Joe ambled over.

A few inches shorter than Tanner and obviously going bald, Joe had kept himself physically fit and looked as strong and athletic as he had fifteen years ago.

"How the heck are ya?" Joe asked, vigorously pumping the hand Tanner extended.

"I'm fine. Actually, I'm glad I ran into you. You're one of the people on my list to call before I move to Florida," Tanner said. "How long has it been, anyway?"

"Would you believe since high school?"

"Yeah, I would believe it," Tanner said. He didn't come home often enough to keep in touch with his friends and he sadly realized that was another casualty of his divorce. "Why weren't you at the dinner last night?"

"The renovation celebration?" Joe asked, frowning.

Tanner nodded.

"Are you kidding? Any self-respecting former jock wouldn't be caught dead at one of those schmaltzy town functions." Joe's eyes narrowed. "You went?"

"My mother made me."

Joe laughed heartily. "No kidding. Your mother made you? Somehow I thought you were one of those guys who stopped listening to his mother long ago."

"Well, typically it's not an issue because she usually stays out of my life."

Tanner made the statement in a matter-of-fact way, but Joe eyed him curiously, and Tanner felt his reputation slip another notch. First Norma saw Bailey turn him down, now Joe knew he still listened to his mother.

Giving Tanner an odd look, Joe asked, "What happened this time?"

"I think she wants grandchildren," Tanner said, deciding he might as well be honest. Events in little Wilmore, West Virginia, really didn't have any impact on the rest of his life. This was a stopover, nothing more. Besides, he was cool. He had always been cool. Even his divorce from Emma hadn't ruined *that* part of his reputation. If he played this right, he could make obeying your mother the hip, trendy thing to do.

Joe laughed. "Oh, you are in trouble."

"It's worse than you think. Not only did I go to the dinner dance, but I actually found someone I liked."

"You lie," Joe said, as if shocked.

Tanner shook his head. "Do you know Bailey Stephenson?"

Joe stared at him. "The beautician?"

Tanner nodded.

"Forget that!" Joe said. "She doesn't go out with anyone."

"Since when have I ever run from a challenge?"

"Never," Joe said. "But Bailey's not a challenge. She's one of those crusader types. Revitalization committee, renovation committee, build a park committee. If there was a division of Save the Whales nearby she'd be on that committee, too.''

"So, she's not avoiding me because she doesn't like me personally?''

"I doubt it. The woman's not interested in anyone and every man who's ever been interested in her ends up on a committee. And after she gets the guy on the committee she keeps him too busy to have time to see her. Nobody's ever figured out how to beat her system.''

"Maybe,'' Tanner proposed, thinking this through as if it were a business deal, not a romantic possibility, ''nobody's ever tried to make the best of the time spent on the committee?''

Joe shook his head. "I don't know. I only know that letting her know you want to take her out is the worst thing you can do. If you like her, the best thing to do is keep it to yourself…'' He stopped to grin. "Of course, if you keep it to yourself, there's no point in being interested, right?

For about thirty seconds silence reigned, then Joe again asked, "Right?''

Tanner knew Joe was looking for Tanner's agreement that the situation was hopeless, but he didn't precisely agree. The trick to getting time with Bailey appeared to be striking a balance. Being in her company because of the committee work and somehow wangling private time to go along with it. To him, the formula was obvious and almost foolproof.

But he didn't like using formulas or trickery of any kind to romance a woman. On top of that, the last thing in the world he needed was to get involved with a crusader. And since he now knew that her justification for not wanting to go out with him was nothing more serious than that she was busy, there was no reason for Tanner

to feel insulted or curious. He really could take no for an
answer.

He really *should* take no for an answer.

But he still had that tingly feeling in the pit of his
stomach that wouldn't leave him alone. He wanted to go
out with her. Really wanted to. Not because there wasn't
anything else to do in this one-horse town, but because
he liked her. He liked the way he felt when he was with
her.

In his teens that was the only reason to go out with a
girl. Because he liked her and liked the way he felt about
himself when he was with her. Being in Wilmore was
bringing all that back for him. The wisdom of his youth.
A sense of self that suddenly felt very comfortable. With
everything in his life changing at a frantic pace, it felt
good to have a kind of order or maybe roots. He wasn't
quite sure how he had turned into the guy who hurt
Emma, but he did know it seemed right to get back to
basics, and he wanted to follow those instincts and in-
tuitions.

The only problem was, the woman he liked didn't want
to see him. Of course, he had already figured out the
formula to fix that. All Tanner had to do was keep her
confused about his purposes for being around her until
she realized he was a nice guy who deserved a date or
two. Hell, if push came to shove, Tanner could find a
branch of Save the Whales and take her to a meeting.
That kind of gesture was exactly what he needed. It
would prove he was benevolent and it would also be a
way to spend time with her.

He glanced at Joe, deciding inside help was standing
right in front of him. Though Joe thought a date with
Bailey was an impossible dream, he had all kinds of facts

at his disposal that Tanner could use to take it from impossible to possible.

He put his arm around Joe's shoulder and led him in the direction of the diner. "Can I buy you lunch?"

"I already ate."

"How about a cup of coffee?"

Joe shrugged. "I could drink a cup."

"Good," Tanner said, then he smiled. He would get Miss Bailey Stephenson to see he was a nice guy. And when he did, she would be glad, because a date with him wasn't exactly torture. Most of the women he dated thought he was fun…interesting…lots of good stuff. This time next week, Bailey would be thanking him.

# Chapter Three

Darkness had descended by the time Bailey arrived at the church hall for the revitalization committee meeting that night. As she had suspected, there was a late-afternoon rush of women who wanted her to remove the pins from their upswept hair and wash out the spray gel that had kept the style alive for over twenty-four hours.

She'd shampooed heads, treasure hunted hairpins and carefully combed out tangles for hours, and she was beat. Sure that the meeting would be over by the time she left the shop, it was only a formality that she drove up the hill to the church. When she saw the lights were still on in the hall, duty and responsibility wouldn't let her turn around and drive away. She parked her SUV, climbed out and headed inside.

The red, white and blue streamers from the celebration the night before were gone and so were the white plastic table covers. All that remained was a utilitarian cement block structure, lit only enough to accommodate the meeting, and furnished with rows of empty tables and green folding chairs.

As she walked through the entryway, she saw Tanner McConnell. Looking like a king holding court with his subjects, he sat at the head of the first long table. The six men in attendance with him made two columns of rapt attention down the table's sides.

When Tanner saw her, he grinned. "Hey, Bailey, come on in."

"Yeah, Bailey, where have you been?" Artie Thorpe asked, sounding annoyed with her.

"I've been shampooing hair. Making a living," she said as she took the seat farthest away from Tanner. She didn't have to be a genius to know what was going on here. He was following her. He couldn't get her to go out with him, so he came to her meeting.

"Tanner has been generous enough to volunteer to be a part of our group until he leaves for Florida," Artie said.

Bailey only gave Tanner a deadpan look, telling him with her expression that she knew what he was doing. Tanner raised his coffee cup as if toasting.

"You missed two hours' worth of his good ideas."

"Oh, they weren't that good," Tanner said, waving away the praise. "The things I told you were just plain old-fashioned business sense, that's all."

"Business sense most of us don't have," Doug McDonald said. And in some way, shape or form everybody at the table agreed with him because they were laborers who worked in the factory in a neighboring city. They weren't company owners or even supervisors at the plant. The only one at the table with any kind of business experience was Bailey. Until Tanner's appearance, she was the one everyone wanted to hear.

"I think we're very lucky to have you here on the committee," Artie said, and that was when Bailey remembered that Artie was married to Tanner's ex-wife. The woman Tanner had left behind. She took a minute to consider that it was generous of Artie to forgive Tanner for hurting Emmalee, then realized Artie wouldn't be married to Em if Tanner hadn't divorced her. And the truth was no one really knew that Tanner hadn't asked Emma to go with him when he left for New York ten years ago. All Emma ever said was that Tanner had moved on to bigger and better things. Everybody assumed he hadn't asked her to move on with him. If he had and she refused, everything about this situation would be backward. Right now it would take great effort for *Tanner* to be nice to Artie, not the other way around.

"So, anyway," Tanner was saying when Bailey came out of her thoughts. "I have to hang around long enough to make sure that the erosion and sedimentation controls are properly installed in the banks of the stream at the back of my parents' property. Then the lane to the house has to be rebuilt." He stopped to laugh. "The flood left ruts and dips that won't go away without the help of several pieces of heavy equipment and about eighteen tons of gravel." He grimaced. "My exhaust system and I found that out the hard way."

"Yeah, too bad about your car," Doug said. "You'll have to talk with Frank in the morning, but I'm pretty sure he doesn't stock Mercedes parts."

"I think you're looking at being in Wilmore at least a month," Artie said, pretending to be sympathetic.

Tanner playfully punched his arm. "Don't kid a kidder. You're glad I'm forced to be around that long because you want my help."

Artie grinned. "I won't lie and say I don't."

"Good," Tanner said. "Then I won't lie and say I'm not flattered that you asked for my help," he added, and Bailey felt a flash of appreciation and respect for Tanner. He might have joined this committee to be with her, but he really did intend to do his part. And not in a condescending fashion, but like one of the team.

Oh, Lord, now he had done it! By joining the committee he tricked her into seeing he was a normal guy, not an icon, not a prince. Just a guy. If she refused to go out with him, she wouldn't be rejecting an image or a personality, she would be rejecting a real person, someone she had to deal with and see at least twice a week for the next three weeks.

Tanner yawned and stretched. "Well, it looks like this good country air has me a little more tired than I'm used to."

"It's the mountains," Doug said.

Tanner nodded. "Probably."

"Let's adjourn the meeting, then," Artie said, rising from his seat.

Though Bailey had been chairperson of the renovation committee, which had been responsible for overseeing flood repairs, everyone had agreed that Artie, as mayor, was a better choice as head of the revitalization committee.

"We'll meet again Wednesday night. Any objections?" he asked, glancing around.

Because Wednesday night was the only weeknight Bailey was available, she certainly didn't have any objections and was grateful when no one else had any, either. They took the adjournment to a vote, it passed unanimously, and everyone started shuffling toward the door.

"Are you ready, Tanner?" Artie asked, fishing his car keys out of his pocket.

"Actually, Artie," Tanner said. "Since Bailey has an SUV it might be better if she took me home. Your van drove in a little low, and that lane really is nothing but ruts and mud pits. I'll just ride home with Bailey." He turned, smiled at her. "You don't mind, do you?"

Doing favors was such a natural thing for Bailey that without thinking she assured him it was no problem. But as soon as the words were out of her mouth, she felt uncomfortable about them. He might be a real person to her now, and he might even be someone willing to help the town, but regardless of how "real" he was or how nice he was, they were still strangers. And he had finagled a ride home with her. Down some of the darkest, loneliest roads in the county.

Her discomfort grew when they headed out of the hall. Most of the group left as soon as the meeting adjourned, and Artie was nowhere around, having gone to turn off the lights. Tanner and Bailey walked through the cement-block entryway alone.

Without giving Bailey a chance to lift her hand to get the doorknob, Tanner reached around her and opened the door. Because she was unaccustomed to such chivalry, she tossed him a puzzled look, and he smiled. Even in the darkened corridor she could see the twinkle in his eyes, the devilment in his grin.

But, oddly, that grin, that symbol of male assurance saved her, because it fueled her determination not to let him get any farther past her defenses than he already had. She refused to be charmed just because he was nice to his ex-wife's new husband, really would help the committee and was endearingly determined to spend time with her. Because, God help her, even his persistence was starting to seem sweet to her. There had never been a man in her life so interested in her that he would go to such lengths just to be in her company…but she wasn't going to let that sway her. She wasn't going to let him charm her. There was no way they could ever have a real relationship and so there was no sense in playing with fire.

She led him to her SUV and unlocked the passenger side door, leaving him no choice but to open it and enter so he could unlock her door for her. Neither said a word while she jumped in, started the engine and pulled out of the parking lot.

"You're not upset with me being on the committee, are you?" Tanner asked.

Because they really needed his help and she was smart enough to know that, she said, "No."

"Well, Artie mentioned that you're the resident expert, since you have a business degree, and I just wanted to make sure you didn't feel like I was usurping your territory."

Surprised that he seemed genuinely concerned that he might have stepped on her toes when that thought had never even occurred to her, Bailey flashed him a quick, assessing look. "This town can use all the help it can get."

"You really believe that, don't you?"

Bailey nodded. "It takes manpower…or womanpower to get the Federal aid, and find the private grants available to accomplish our special projects. For twenty years we sat back and settled for what we could afford from taxes, and when the flood came we realized it wasn't much. But the flood was an unexpected blessing, too, because it forced us to apply for Federal money for disaster aid. Now that everybody's accustomed to dealing with the government, we're not as inhibited as we had been. And we're not afraid to go after more, to take the next steps. We have a chance to propel ourselves into the twenty-first century. I want to take it."

"Well, I'm behind you 100 percent."

"Really?" she asked, happy to give him the benefit of the doubt. They sure as heck could use his assistance.

"Really," he confirmed, but as soon as he said it she remembered he was leaving. And soon. He wouldn't be around to see any of these projects through to completion. She suddenly worried that his popping onto the committee for a few weeks might do more harm than good.

Maneuvering her vehicle onto the rut-filled lane that led to his parents' small farm, she said, "I'm just a little bit concerned that everybody's going to be disappointed when you leave."

"Are you speaking for the committee now, or for yourself?"

Again she cast him a quick, assessing glance. The dim light from the dashboard barely illuminated his handsome face and his short sandy brown hair that was carefully styled to look careless and natural. He had those classic boy-next-door good looks. Light brown hair streaked with yellow by the sun, big green eyes, sun-tanned skin. And at the meeting he had shown her that he could be nice. Considerate. Fair.

Part of her actually wished she could be honest and tell him that she didn't want to get involved with him because he would leave her and any woman would miss a man like him when he was gone. But if she turned this into a personal discussion, she'd lose the opportunity to explain the very serious concerns she had about him jumping in to help only to disappear in a few weeks.

Using her most patient voice, she said, "Tanner, this town needs help, and these guys respect and like you enough that they're willing to humble themselves and admit that they don't know what their next steps should be. I'm afraid if they humble themselves too far, depend on you too much, they'll lose the confidence it took them all spring to build. And when you're gone I'll be starting from scratch again. Cheerleading to make them believe they can do all this. But more than that, this isn't like the big city where volunteers are a dime a dozen. If you start a hundred projects then leave in the middle of them, we could very well be stranded.''

Her last statement took them to the end of the lane, almost to the bottom step of his parents' front porch. She jerked the gearshift into park, and faced him, because really that was the bottom line. Not just to his being on the committee, but to his being in her life. ''To you this might be noble and sort of fun for the moment, but I'm the one who's going to be left picking up the pieces or trying to hold everything together when you leave.''

''I won't leave in the middle of something,'' he said, capturing her gaze, looking like he was talking more about them personally, than the town or the committee and its problems. ''And I won't start something that I can't finish.''

''Getting the funding for some of these projects will take years,'' Bailey protested over the ripple of yearning that swept through her at his sincere voice, the honesty in his simple words. She genuinely believed he didn't understand what he was dragging her or her poor town into. ''You're not going to hang around for years.''

''No,'' he agreed, shaking his head to emphasize it. ''But there are telephones and fax machines and even e-mail and instant messages. If you want to communicate with someone badly enough, you can.''

That made her laugh. ''I'm about the only one in this

town who has e-mail and even knows what an instant message is.''

''You're the only one I care about.''

Her head shot up and she stared at him. Though he had hovered around the fine line between talking about the committee and talking about her, with that comment he crossed over. Fear nearly paralyzed her. No matter how cute he was, how sincere he sounded, how nice he was to the people on her committee, or even how much she wanted this, she absolutely, positively could not get involved with this man. He was leaving. She was staying. They were a disaster waiting to happen. She would not willfully put herself in a position of getting hurt. That would be insanity.

But before she could say anything, he said, ''You know what I mean.'' Then he grinned and yanked on the handle of the passenger side door. ''As long as there is one person to contact, I can be in touch. This isn't hard, Bailey. Don't make it hard.''

With that he jumped out and slammed her car door. Bailey waited until he was inside the house before she put her gearshift into drive and bounced her way out of his parents' lane, feeling oddly empty. But she had done the right thing. She knew she had done the right thing.

It wasn't until she was at the door of her apartment that she realized he hadn't made a move to kiss her. And he hadn't actually flirted with her, either. Most of the time she thought he might have been talking about a relationship with her, he could have been talking about the committee. All he had really done was confuse her.

Or maybe she had confused herself. Since he hadn't kissed her or tried, hadn't asked her out or tried. Maybe she was only complimenting herself to think he joined the committee to be with her.

\* \* \*

"Cora, I'm telling you it was the most confusing situation I've ever been in."

"I don't see how," Cora Beth Johnson said, balancing her fist on her right hip as she stared at Bailey. Tall, thin, brown-eyed Cora had been Bailey's best friend since grade school and now was her best employee. The two were supposed to be doing a late-Monday-night inventory before a salesman arrived Tuesday morning, but so far all Cora had done was stand and stare at Bailey.

"Well, you know, we were talking about the committee. Talking about things that need to be done and how disappointing it will be if Tanner leaves. Devastating, really," Bailey said, catching Cora's gaze. "And he acted like I was making a mountain out of a molehill."

"I think you are."

Bailey shook her head vigorously. "Don't you see? He's going to get us into things that we don't have the manpower to handle."

"Are you saying that he can somehow do the work of three people and that when he leaves we'll be short-handed?"

"No, I'm saying that his experience and expertise can open a lot of doors for us and get us to the places we need to go, but when he sets out for Florida we'll be left hanging."

"I don't see why," Cora said. "Your whole reason for the revitalization committee was to keep our foot in the Federal Government's door. It sounds to me like Tanner's connections might be able to open the door a little wider, or a little faster, but that's about all."

"And that's the point," Bailey said. "He'll get the doors open and leave us twisting in the wind."

Cora gaped at Bailey. "The people of this town are

not overly educated, but they aren't stupid. If Tanner stays around long enough to open the doors wider, we'll catch on to how to keep them open."

Bailey sighed. "I suppose."

"I know you know I'm right. That answer is too obvious for a smart woman like you to have missed it. And you have a lot of faith in the people of this town, so I also know you recognize that we'll get by somehow," Cora Beth said, studying Bailey. "So what's really bothering you?"

"I don't know."

"Come on," Cora said, playfully nudging Bailey. "We've been best friends for almost two decades. I'm the one who talked you into going to beauty school after you got your degree so you could buy this business and start a chain of your own salons. I know you like the back of my hand. I love you like a sister. If you can't tell me, who can you tell?"

Licking her dry lips, Bailey nodded. "You're right. If I can't tell you there's no one I can tell."

"So what's the scoop?"

"Do you remember how Norma started that rumor about Tanner McConnell being interested in me?"

Cora nodded.

"Well, I don't think it's a rumor."

Cora cocked her head in question. "You don't *think?*"

"Yeah, I don't *think*. And only *think* because I really don't know."

"How can you not know that a man is interested in you?"

"Because I don't. Until last night I thought he was. He's asked me out. In fact, he was asking me out when Norma came in, but I turned him down."

"You turned him down?" Cora echoed through a gasp.

"He's leaving, Cora..."

"Well, shoot, I know that, but just like with the revitalization committee, a little Tanner McConnell goes a long way. You take what you can get and worry about tomorrow, tomorrow."

"That's just it. I don't worry about tomorrow, tomorrow. I worry about tomorrow today. That's what businesspeople do."

"So, you won't go out with him because someday he'll be leaving?"

"Precisely."

Cora only stared at her friend. "You are nuts."

"No. I'm smart. I'm avoiding getting hurt."

"Who says he's going to hurt you?" Cora challenged.

"How could it possibly not hurt when he leaves?" Bailey countered, then busied herself with finishing her supply inventory because it was getting late and the conversation was getting uncomfortable.

"Maybe he'll take you with him."

For that Bailey peeked at Cora. "I wouldn't want to go."

Cora's mouth dropped open on another gasp. "What in the hell are you talking about now?"

"Don't you see? I couldn't go. How could I? If we both deserted the revitalization committee, we'd be leaving everybody holding the bag."

Cora leaned against the countertop. "Let me get this straight. You won't date Tanner McConnell...*the* Tanner McConnell because you don't want to desert the town."

"Yes. That and the fact that I'm not sure he would take me with him. After all, he left Emmalee behind."

"You're judging him on a bunch of things that happened ten years ago?" Cora asked incredulously.

"You don't think it's right to judge a person by his past behavior?" Bailey asked, equally incredulous.

"No!" Cora protested. "First, no one really knows the whole story behind his breakup with Emmalee. But, second, ten long years have passed. The man owned a company. Even if he didn't want to take Emma with him because he was acting too big for his britches, I'm just about certain he's over that by now. Everybody grows up sometime, Bailey."

"Maybe," Bailey conceded with a nod.

"But you don't want to be the person who gives him a break?"

"Cora, I don't want to give my *heart* a break. I have a business to run. And he's already interfering in my life. I think he only joined the revitalization committee to show me he's a good guy. To get me to go out with him."

"Okay," Cora said, holding up her hands to stop Bailey. "Again, I'm having trouble understanding the problem. Even if he only did join that committee to get a date, if he stays long enough to help us out, you've inadvertently solved some of the town's biggest problems just by getting him to work for us for a while." Cora paused, then grinned. "In fact, if you play your cards right, when he does announce that he's leaving, you could say yes to a date and get him to stay a few weeks longer. Maybe even a couple of months."

Bailey sighed. "Now I think you're making fun of me."

"Oh, I'm not making fun of you, sugar," Cora said, sliding her arm across Bailey's shoulders. "Well, maybe a little. But you have to admit it all sounds odd. The most handsome man we know wants to date you and you tell him no. But you say he can't take no for an answer, when he has probably hundreds of other women to choose from. So you think he joined a two-bit committee to help his hometown, not because he's a generous man with time on his hands, but to get to know you.''

"When you put it that way, it does sound ridiculous."

"Yes, it does," Cora said, not even trying to be nice anymore because, Bailey knew, she was trying to drive her point home.

Bailey sighed. "Okay, I get it. I'm being ridiculous."

"When you *should* be very, very nice to Tanner McConnell," Cora sternly reminded Bailey. "Honey, these are your pet projects he'll be working on. He might help for a month or two and get a lot of the credit, but you're going to be around forever. You'll be here to jog on that trail through the woods and ride your bike on the bike path. Your kids will go to the community college, and you and I will play bingo at the Senior Center. We should be kissing this man's feet."

"You're right," Bailey said, suddenly feeling foolish.

The bell above the salon door rang. Bailey and Cora looked at each other.

"Who could that be?" Cora whispered.

"I don't know," Bailey said.

"Hello? Anybody here?" Tanner called out.

Cora and Bailey exchanged another glance, then Cora said, "Back here, Tanner," before she turned to Bailey and whispered, "You be nice to him."

Bailey drew a resigned breath. "Right. You're right. I've been foolish and strange about this whole deal. I'll settle down now."

"Good," Cora said, then took off her smock and

straightened her T-shirt over her jeans. "Since you don't want him, maybe I'll have a crack at this."

"Cora, the man is leaving…"

Cora smiled. "And with any luck, I'll be going with him."

"Whatever." Bailey rolled her eyes as she and Cora left the supply room.

"Hey, Tanner," Bailey said, leading Cora into the salon. "We were in the back doing inventory."

Tanner smiled at her. "I know. Joe told me. I was wondering if you could give me a ride home. When I took my car to the garage this morning, Frank confirmed what Doug had said. He doesn't stock Mercedes parts. He guesses it will be at least three weeks until he gets the parts in." He spread his hands helplessly. "So, I'm at the mercy of free rides."

"But you're here for three weeks," Cora put in, glancing at Bailey.

"At least," Tanner said, giving Cora a smile that would probably make her swoon internally. "I sold my business," he explained unnecessarily; everybody in town knew he had. "And I'm not going to start the new one until I've had a few months off." He paused long enough to shrug. "Who knows? I might end up staying here six months."

With that added piece of information, Cora's smile grew. "I'll be glad to give you a ride home," she said, her voice light and lilting and obviously flirtatious.

"Well, thank you, Cora Beth," Tanner said. His use of her middle name reminded Bailey that Tanner had been friends with Cora's brother, Joe. The same Joe who would have told him that she and Cora would be doing inventory. The same Joe he bumped into Sunday morning when he left her salon. The same Joe who'd probably told Tanner quite a lot. Wondering what else Joe might have told Tanner, Bailey narrowed her eyes as Tanner continued. "But Bailey has an SUV. I won't even drive my father's car out of that lane, it's so bad. At least with Bailey I know I won't be causing someone to rip up a muffler or exhaust system."

"He's right," Bailey said, taking Cora's advice to be nice to him, but also deciding she was correct about Tanner's intentions. Tanner might not have kissed her or even made personal conversation with her on the way home from the meeting, but he was still interested. She was sure of it. She couldn't figure out what Joe might have told him to get him to shift from determined suitor to "friend," but whatever it was, technically, it worked in her favor. Because, as Cora pointed out, she now had a well-connected, intelligent man on her committee. And, since Tanner's interest in her was no longer apparent, women like Cora Beth felt free to pursue him. Eventually he would get tired of being nice to Bailey with no results and switch to a more responsive woman. Bailey was sure of it.

She smiled at him. "I'll be glad to take you home. In fact, Cora and I were just about finished. Why don't you go to my dad's bar and grab a beer and when we're done, I'll come by and get you."

Tanner shook his head. "No. Waiting here is fine. I don't want to be any trouble."

"You're no trouble," Cora insisted, helping him to a seat along the wall where patrons waited their turn for a haircut.

"Can I get you a magazine?"

Tanner glanced at the contents of the wicker table beside his chair and he chuckled. "I don't think I'm quite ready to read *Cosmo* yet."

Cora laughed. Bailey decided to leave her friend to her own devices while she returned to the supply room to finish taking inventory. After fifteen minutes, the order for the salesman was written. She walked back into the salon to find Cora laughing outrageously with Tanner.

Something akin to jealousy rose up in her, but she stopped it. First of all, she had already turned down Tanner when he asked her out. Second, she really didn't want a broken heart. Third, Cora probably had more right to like him than Bailey did. Because Cora and Tanner had background information on each other and a history of sorts, in a few weeks they could form the kind of relationship that would allow Tanner to ask her to leave with him. Bailey had no right to want to stop that.

After closing the shop and saying goodbye to Cora, Bailey and Tanner walked to her SUV in complete silence. As she had done the night before, she unlocked his door first, so he couldn't do something gentlemanly like open her door.

But when she slid in behind the wheel, he said, "What's up?"

Shoving her key into the ignition, she glanced at him. "What do you mean, 'What's up?'"

"You're acting odd. Did something happen? Did I do something?"

"No," she said brightly, remembering what Cora had said about not offending him. "I guess if I'm acting weird it's because I had a long talk with Cora tonight and decided I had jumped the gun with some of the things I had said to you when I drove you home after the meeting. It was presumptuous of me to think you would leave us in the lurch. I need to apologize."

"Apology accepted. It's a relief to hear you realize you were wrong about me helping," Tanner said as Bailey maneuvered her vehicle onto the quiet main street of the now-sleeping town. "Because I want to help. I have time on my hands and expertise. It's not a problem."

Neither of them said anything as she drove through town, but when she pulled onto the dark, deserted road to his parents' home, Tanner suddenly started to laugh.

"What's funny?"

"You were talking about me," he said, but in a tone to indicate that the thought pleased him enormously.

"What?"

"You were talking about me," Tanner repeated. "You and Cora were talking about me."

"I was talking about your helping the town."

"Doesn't matter," Tanner said, then chuckled again. "You were still talking about me, and I'm flattered."

Bailey gave him a patient look, but her heart fluttered and her pulse raced. She had been talking about him, and for just the reasons he suspected. He confused her and intrigued her enough that she'd sought guidance from a friend. "Don't be flattered. We were discussing the town."

He tapped his index finger on her nose. "You were discussing me." He glanced out the window, then back at Bailey. "So what were you talking about?"

"About you helping the town," Bailey reiterated, trying to be patient and failing miserably.

"No, that might have gotten it started, but you went farther, I can tell. Otherwise, Cora would have flirted with me."

Bailey's mouth dropped open. "She *was* flirting with you!"

"Oh…and you were jealous," Tanner said as if he had just figured it out. "That's why you hardly said anything when we walked to the car."

"That is not why I hardly said anything when we were walking to the car," Bailey insisted, but she knew that wasn't true. Theoretically she had been quiet with him because she didn't know what to say now that Cora Beth was interested in him. So in a way he was right, even though technically he wasn't. And now she was so confused she didn't know what to say.

"Well, I'm not interested in Cora Beth," Tanner said suddenly, his words tiptoeing into the vehicle which, though quiet, seemed to crackle with something Bailey couldn't identify. "She's like a little sister to me. Hell, I helped Joe beat the heck out of some guy who was spreading rumors about her love life. I could never go out with Cora."

The rest of the drive, including the bumpy trip down the muddy lane, was made in complete silence. When Bailey stopped the car in front of his parents' house, Tanner didn't jump out as she expected him to do. Instead he reached over and snapped off her engine, then just as quickly he removed the keys and tucked them into his front pants pocket.

"Hey!" Bailey yelped, but it was too late. If she went after her keys she would get herself into much bigger trouble than she was already.

"The only woman I'm interested in in this town is you," he said softly, quietly, completely ignoring her protests about her keys. "But you won't go out with me because you don't seem to like me. You forced me into the position of ruining my exhaust system and joining a committee."

Bailey gasped. "So, I was right. You did join that committee because of me!"

Tanner looked at Bailey and grinned. "Shoot me."

"Shoot you!" Bailey parroted, exasperated. "I should

shoot you. I now know you well enough to recognize that you would never take advantage of a woman, but you should be smart enough to take no for an answer—''

"See," Tanner said proudly. "I already accomplished my first objective. You're getting to know me. Soon you'll know me well enough that you won't have any excuse not to go out with me."

"Oh, Tanner," Bailey said, but it came out more like a groan. "This just isn't going to work. I'm not like the usual fluff chickens you date. I'm not impressed with this kind of stuff."

"Then what does impress you?" he asked quietly.

She shrugged. "I don't know."

"Well, let's try looking at it from another angle. Has any man ever impressed you?"

She thought for a minute, then shook her head. "Not really. I'm sort of a workaholic, so I don't go out much."

"Yeah, I know that feeling," Tanner said, stretching his legs out as he leaned back on her seat. "I worked sixteen hours a day when I started my business. Some days I worked eighteen or twenty. If you're interested in making a franchise out of your salon, you might as well get ready to work your butt off, too."

"How did you know I was planning to make my salon a franchise?"

He glanced at her. "Aren't you?"

"Yeah, but that's not the kind of thing you could guess—" She stopped, remembered that she had seen him with Joe Sunday morning, and she laughed. "You were talking about me, too!"

He shrugged. "Yeah, so what? I like you and have the guts enough to admit it. In fact," he said, shifting on the seat until he was facing her. "I like you enough that I'm going to kiss you."

As he said the last he slid his hand behind her neck, under her hair, and nudged her forward slightly. At first Bailey was so stunned she didn't know what to do, but she suddenly realized that he was taking his time, going very slowly to give her the opportunity to stop him or to make some kind of protest.

She almost told him to stop, but the words died in her throat. Looking into his gorgeous green eyes, feeling his fingers on her nape, and being drawn into intimate proximity, Bailey discovered she wanted to kiss him. Not only was she abundantly curious, not only did she agree with Cora that he probably had grown and matured since his marriage to Emma, but no matter what she said or how she protested, his stepping in to help her favorite cause really had impressed her. He wasn't anything like what she thought he would be.

And, yeah, she wanted to kiss him.

# Chapter Four

When Bailey didn't protest, Tanner froze. He didn't expect to get to kiss her tonight. He thought for sure she would stop him. When she didn't, the recognition that she was attracted to him enough to *want* to kiss him shot a ripple of arousal through him. Again, like the night he met her, he had an involuntary reaction. The spontaneity sweetened the pot, hitching the excitement a notch, urging him on to take everything he could get in this unexpected opportunity. He edged closer, sliding across the seat at the same time that he nudged her into shifting a little nearer. And, the entire time, they stared into each other's eyes.

Looking at the unusual violet color of her eyes, which were large and round with anticipation, Tanner had the sense that they were embarking on something monumental. He felt the softness of her cheek against the heel of his hand and the satiny caress of her hair entwined in his fingers, and sensation after sensation buffeted him. Instinct after instinct clamored for attention. He thought of a hundred reasons to make love to her right here, right now. But he realized that even if she let him, it would be the first and last time he would have her. She would never let herself be vulnerable around him again. He would probably never be alone with her again.

The thought left him unexpectedly devastated. He wanted more from her than a good-night kiss. He wanted her to trust him, respect him and spend time with him. He wouldn't get that if he took advantage of her now.

He slid his hand out from under her hair and shifted away from her. "I want to kiss you, but I'm not going to," he said, tossing her keys to her and grabbing the handle of the door before he changed his mind. Needs he didn't know he could possess rose up in him and caused him to catch her gaze again. "I want you to trust me. I want you to like me. When I kiss you I want to know I'm getting every part of you, not just the part that's grateful and maybe the part that's curious about me. I want every part."

With that he opened the door and stepped out into the June night, which seemed very cold compared to the temperature of the SUV. He jogged up his parents' steps absolutely positive he was out of his league with this woman, this relationship, and equally positive he was crazy for not taking what he could get when he could get it and walking away like he usually did.

Bailey entered the beauty shop the next morning with bloodshot eyes and a tingle in her stomach that wouldn't seem to leave. She had never had a man take her to the brink of arousal just by threatening to kiss her. She'd never had a man's refusal to kiss her boost that arousal into full-scale yearning.

Tanner McConnell was driving her nuts.

Cora Beth virtually ran into the shop. Wide-eyed and out of breath, she asked, "So what happened?"

Bailey shook out the smock she had left hanging on her salon chair the night before. "Nothing," she answered honestly.

Cora groaned. "Come on. I can tell something happened. Did he kiss you?"

Bailey only stared at her friend. "Cora, I thought *you* were interested in him."

"I am. But in the same way that somebody plays the lottery. I know I'm not the only person who has a ticket."

Bailey started for the office behind the salon. "You're crazy."

"No, you're crazy," Cora countered, following her. "I'm guessing he tried to kiss you and you stopped him."

"Well, you would be wrong."

"You let him kiss you?" Cora asked on a happy gasp.

Bailey shook her head. "He didn't kiss me."

Confused, Cora Beth stopped dead in her tracks. "No one got kissed because no one tried to kiss anybody else?"

"Essentially," Bailey said. Though she knew that wasn't precisely the truth, but it was better than having to explain something she didn't understand herself.

"So maybe he doesn't like you," Cora said, still sounding puzzled.

"Cora, life doesn't boil down to sound bites. You don't take one look at a person and decide you want to marry them. You don't sleep with or kiss every man you meet simply because you can. People are supposed to think about things. To make rational decisions."

Which was what she'd told herself the night before. Tanner hadn't kissed her because he had made a rational decision to reach for something more. He wanted her to trust him. He wanted her to like him. When he kissed her, he wanted to know he was getting every part of her.

Just repeating his words in her head shot a shiver through her.

And made her nervous. The things he said made her nervous and she refused to deny it. She had instincts and longings about the man that she had never had with anyone. Part of her wanted to follow them. Part knew it was fruitless. If Tanner was getting the intuition to go slowly and be careful, it might be because he also recognized that what they wanted and what they could have were two different things.

Which took her right back to the beginning. She might like him. He might be the most attractive man on the face of the earth. But they had no future. And people who dabbled in temporary relationships got hurt.

She knew that from personal experience.

But when she saw him Wednesday night in the cement-block foyer of the church hall, all her senses went on red alert. Just being in the same room with him made her tingle.

"Hi," she said, then almost cursed herself because she sounded young and breathless, as if she had been counting the minutes until she saw him again.

He smiled. "Hi."

She knew the greeting was intended to be casual and friendly but because of the things he had said to her in her car there was an intimacy between them that turned that one simple word into something like a caress. He liked her. He wanted her. He wanted more from her than simple kisses.

Knowing all that, gazing into his beautiful green eyes,

pinpricks of awareness floated through her. "We should sit," she said, but she didn't release his gaze.

He continued to stare at her as he said, "Yeah, I think Artie's about ready to start the meeting." Then he closed his eyes and took a quick breath. "You're late again."

She knew he made the pointless comment because they couldn't go into a meeting full of townspeople looking starry-eyed and bemused, and thirty seconds of normal, sane conversation would take away all traces of questionable behavior.

She nodded and followed his lead. "No matter how hard you plan and how concisely you schedule, it only takes one late person or one hard-to-curl head of hair to throw a monkey wrench in everything."

"You see, the same was true with my trucking company," Tanner said, sounding amazed at how such diametrically opposed businesses could be so similar. "A flat tire, a slow stream of traffic, too many red lights, any number of little, ordinary things could ruin a perfectly good day."

"Is that why you sold your business?" Bailey asked, hardly realizing that he was pulling out a chair for her at the table full of men preoccupied with their own conversations.

He shook his head as he sat beside her. "No. I enjoyed working. I *will* work in Florida when I start the charter fishing business. The truth is somebody offered me a great deal of money for my company, and I had the instinct that this was the time to get out of one business and shift into another."

"You put a lot of stock in instinct," Bailey said, knowing that was why he hadn't kissed her.

He shook his head. "Would you believe I've only started to do that recently? Until now I've been a rather straightforward, stick-to-the-rules businessman. Now," he said, catching her gaze, sending a shaft of awareness through her, "everything seems to have changed."

"I would like to call this meeting to order," Artie said, pounding a meat mallet, which they were using as a gavel of sorts, and preventing Bailey from answering. "As is our usual practice, you have a typewritten copy of the minutes in front of you from the last meeting. So, unless somebody has a question on any of that, I say we approve the minutes from that meeting and move forward with this one."

Everybody mumbled an agreement, and Artie continued.

"To update you on our progress..." he began, then proceeded to explain the results of some of the phone calls he had made to set the wheels in motion for a few of their projects. His update took about ten minutes, but the discussions of where they needed to go from here took an entire hour.

When everything seemed to have died down, Tanner said, "I made a few calls myself."

"You did?" Artie said hopefully, obviously not only recognizing that his own efforts were small potatoes, but also that they were woefully slow. If Tanner was welcome on this committee for one reason, it was to plow through red tape.

"Yeah," Tanner said, grinning. "And I found a private group that funds parks."

"What?" Bailey asked, not quite sure she had heard correctly.

"There is a wealthy family in Virginia by the name of Smith, who has a foundation. The sole purpose of their foundation is to give money to small towns that want to build or renovate parks. Supposedly the application process is very simple, and rumor has it that if you get approved, you sometimes get a check the same day.''

Bailey stared at him. "You're kidding?"

He shook his head. "It's a private foundation, Bailey. They can do anything they want. But because they have a lot of money at their disposal and they're trying to be careful with it, they also don't do things in a loud or obvious way. It takes effort to find them…"

"But you found them in three days," Bailey said incredulously.

"I have an enormous friend base and some terrific pull with a few people in government," he said, grinning. "Come on, Bailey, let me finish. If we play our cards right, this family will completely fund the new park. Better yet, if we present the petition correctly, we could call your bike trail a park and get money for that, too."

"In three days," Bailey said, falling backward on her seat with a thump, "you did what we couldn't do in three months."

"I'm invaluable," Tanner teased.

But Bailey only blinked at him. "I can't believe this."

As if coming out of a state of shock, the rest of the group offered hearty congratulations and broke into little sections of buzzing conversation. Flabbergasted, Bailey realized that she had no worry about Tanner leaving town before his work was done. One way or another he would get it done. She also realized that a lot of the tasks and maneuvering necessary to find the money they needed probably looked easy to him. And then she realized she owed him. The whole town owed him. And they shouldn't be so quick to judge him anymore.

"There's only one thing," Tanner said slowly, breaking into the jubilation. "We have to impress the family."

"We can do that!" Doug McDonald crowed triumphantly. "We're sincere, honest people. We can impress a *family*."

"Well, this family isn't like any that you've met," Tanner explained slowly. "In fact, the family matriarch is supposed to be...well, crazy. And she controls the fund."

"I knew there was a catch," Artie mumbled dispiritedly.

"Not that much of a catch," Tanner insisted. "Look, when I was in the trucking business I did things like this all the time. I went after work no one else wanted. Usually no one wanted it because there was one difficult element to the job. So all I had to do was figure out how to minimize the problem, and I ended up making lots of money. Which is what we have to do right now. Try to uncover what it is that this woman wants from the towns to which she gives money, and then prove we have it. You just have to have faith that we can do this."

"And you think we can?"

"I've already made arrangements for Bailey and me to meet with Mrs. Smith, since I think she and I are the most logical people to scope out the situation. If Mrs. Smith is so incredibly unmanageable that we can't see how we would deal with her, we can back out without expending too much time or effort and look for another trust or foundation to help us. But if she's just a little old woman with a bad reputation, we pounce."

"Okay, sounds reasonable to me," Artie said.

"It is reasonable. And much faster than trying to get money from the government." He turned to Bailey. "Are you with me?"

"Sure," Bailey said. She understood what he was doing. To get things done quickly they might have to use unorthodox means, but one success would shift momentum. If they could get the park, that would bring the enthusiasm of the entire town behind them to support them as they labored toward the more difficult tasks and funding...like the community college. "Yes, I'm with you."

"Good, we leave for Virginia tomorrow."

"Great!" Artie said, beaming, and Bailey could tell he understood the same things she did about momentum and enthusiasm. "Since that kind of puts everything else on the back burner, I say we adjourn and set a meeting for Friday. You'll be back by Friday night, right?"

"I would say we won't need to stay more than a day or two," Tanner responded.

Bailey blinked. "A day or two?"

Tanner faced her slowly. "Yeah. We meet her tomorrow for lunch and try to get her to see us again as quickly as possible. If she can't see us, we'll come home. But if she wants to meet with us again tomorrow night, or Friday sometime, we would be crazy to turn her down."

"I have a business to run," Bailey said incredulously.

"Can't Cora Beth fill in?"

"Cora Beth has her own customers."

"There isn't anybody who can do this for us...for the town?"

Bailey drew a long breath. Her objection wasn't so much that she needed a replacement; she had a new stylist who could handle the flow of weekday haircuts under Cora's supervision. The problem was he hadn't consulted her before he made these plans.

No, the problem was she didn't want to be out of town with a man who made her want to melt into a puddle at his feet, and Tanner knew that. That was why he hadn't consulted her before he made these plans. She was also worried that his definition of wanting "more" from her and their relationship might include things for which she wasn't anywhere near ready.

"Look," Tanner said. "Don't worry about it. There's nothing definite here. I shouldn't have arranged this without giving you time to straighten out your work schedule. I'll just call her back and tell her we'll meet with her another time." He paused, considered the situation, then said, "Or I could go myself. Yeah, I'll go myself. There's really no need for two of us."

"Or I could go," Artie suggested.

Tanner shook his head. "I'm fine. I've done things like this a hundred times. I just thought Bailey's enthusiasm for the town would help sway Mrs. Smith. But what I don't have in understanding I make up for with charm." He grinned. "I'll be fine."

"Damn right you will," Doug said with a laugh.

"Okay, then, it's settled," Artie said, pounding the meat mallet. "Meeting adjourned."

The sound of chairs scraping across the floor as they were pulled away from the table filled the air. Tanner turned to Bailey. "Give me a ride home?"

She shrugged. "Sure," she said, but she felt like an idiot. If it had been anybody else but Tanner who had made the suggestion that she go to Virginia on a mission for the town, she would have handled her business problems to make time for the trip in a second. But by letting her personal confusion about the man get in the way, she was letting the town down.

She waited until they were almost at his parents' lane before she said, "I'll go to Virginia with you."

He brushed her offer aside. "Nah, don't worry about it. This is a first meeting. I'll scope her out, come home, and then we'll plan a strategy." He paused long enough to catch her gaze. "I think I jumped the gun. You know, pushing too hard too fast for too much. I shouldn't have done that. I'm a patient man. I don't need to push."

Little prickles of excitement raced up her arm, giving her chills. He had a luxurious, masculine voice, but it wasn't his voice that thrilled her. It was that he always said the most wonderful things. Not only had he just told her he respected her right to go slowly while she waded through all these brand-new feelings he incited in her, but he'd also proven he wouldn't embarrass her by accusing her of thinking he had set this trip up to seduce her. He knew that was what she thought, because that's what it looked like. But it appeared that in his enthusiasm to do right by the committee, he had inadvertently forced her into a corner, and now he was working to fix that mistake. He was going out of his way to make sure she knew she could trust him, that it genuinely was a mistake, and he would be more careful in the future.

"I'm going."

He peeked at her as she maneuvered her vehicle down the bumpy lane. "Really? You're sure?"

"I'm positive," she said through a groan. "I've seen the need for the park, the college and even the senior center for years. It took a flood to get the town support I needed to go after funding. I would be a fool to pass up this opportunity."

"Yes, you would," he agreed as she brought the SUV to a stop at the foot of the steps to his parents' front porch. "But you wouldn't be passing up the opportunity, you would just be delaying it somewhat."

"I don't want to delay it."

He caught her gaze again. "Sometimes delays are good things."

"I know," she said, then licked her suddenly dry lips because she realized what he was telling her. If his going alone was the cost of convincing her he hadn't tried to force her into a situation for which she wasn't ready, he would go alone because more than anything else he wanted her to trust him. He had come right out and said that the night he refused to kiss her.

"And I trust you," she added softly.

He wrapped his fingers around the door handle but otherwise didn't make a move to leave. Bailey realized that in admitting she trusted him she had overcome his reason for not kissing her. If he kissed her now, he would have her completely, different from on Monday night. Because this kiss wouldn't be an experiment. This kiss would be a confirmation that they had moved to the next level of their relationship. She trusted him; he could kiss her.

As she thought the last, a shiver of awareness shot through her. Tanner looked at her. He held her eyes captive for several seconds before dropping his gaze to her mouth and then bringing it back to her eyes again. The moment seemed to stretch on for eternity. Bailey could swear her heart would beat out of her chest. Her lips tingled in anticipation. She had never wanted to kiss anyone as much as she wanted to kiss Tanner McConnell right now, but because he wasn't making the move, she knew he still had doubts.

She could resolve his doubts just by stretching forward and pressing her lips to his. One soft kiss from her would confirm that she really did trust him, that she liked him and that a kiss was their mutual idea. But before she could get her muscles to make the moves her brain was commanding, he jerked on the door handle.

"Thanks for the ride," he said, then jumped out of her SUV and slammed the door.

Bailey slumped on her seat.

* * *

"You're about to go out of town with the man," Cora said, sighing with exasperation.

Cora had been waiting for Bailey when Bailey arrived at the shop. And unlike the day before, this time Bailey gave details. It was embarrassing to reveal that she was absolutely positive Tanner was going to kiss her but didn't, and even more embarrassing to admit that she had no clue what was going on and she needed guidance.

"You might even be staying overnight," Cora said. "Of course, he's not going to make a romantic overture and scare you to death. He's honorable, Bailey. That's why a lot of us didn't buy the obvious gossip that he had dumped Emma without a backward glance. It's also why most of us like him." She paused, considered, then added, "That and the fact that he's absolutely gorgeous."

"He does seem to be an honorable guy," Bailey agreed as she continued to arrange the curlers on her section of the counter in anticipation of her first customer of the morning, Mrs. Woodside, who wanted a perm. Having only been fifteen when Tanner divorced his wife, Bailey hadn't paid too much attention to what had gone on, only heard the rumors, processed them and didn't really care. But Cora knew Tanner because he was friends with her brother. If Cora thought he was honest, then he was probably honest.

"Tanner has always been a nice guy," Cora said, fixing her own hair before their customers arrived.

"And you don't think he just left Emma behind like she wasn't good enough for him anymore?"

Cora shrugged. "I don't know. He's never talked about it, but it was ten years ago. Even if he did leave Emma behind, he's ten years older. I'm sure he's changed. He *looks* changed," she insisted. Then she sighed. "I've known both of you since I was a little girl. I like you both. If you asked me, you're a match made in heaven."

"Actually, Cora, that's the problem," Bailey said. "I don't think we're a match."

Cora stared at her. "You don't?"

"No. I know we like each other. I know we're very attracted to each other, but all you have to do is listen to us talk to realize our lives are going in two different directions."

"I don't understand," Cora said.

"It's very simple," Bailey said. "He's moving to Florida. He's buying a big boat. He's taking fishing parties out to sea. He sees it in his head. I can tell."

"And it sounds like a fun adventure. Who says you wouldn't enjoy that?"

"Who says I would?" Bailey demanded. "And who says I even want to try? Look around you, Cora. You talked me into getting my beautician's license and buying this shop. I want to use my brain and make something of my life. I don't want to be somebody's little fluff chicken, giving tours off the Florida coast. Don't you see? We are not a match made in heaven!"

"All right," Cora said, stepping back as if Bailey had insulted her. "You don't have to yell about it."

"I'm sorry," Bailey said, turning away from her friend, hoping the discussion would end. Because the truth was she *was* sorry. Tanner McConnell was the first man she had been attracted to since college. It felt unfair that they would have such different life goals. In fact, it infuriated her, and that's what bothered her. Normally she could look at a situation, reason out whether it was right or wrong and then make a logical choice, and her heart would fall in line.

This time her heart wanted to race ahead of the logical choice, but Bailey knew she couldn't. The one and only time she had done that, she had not only gotten hurt, she'd lost everything.

# Chapter Five

At six o'clock the next morning, Tanner sat on the porch swing and watched Bailey drive down the lane of his parents' home to pick him up for their meeting with Mrs. Smith. As she pulled her SUV up to the steps, he rose. By the time her vehicle had come to a complete stop, he was at the door.

He opened it, jumped inside and smiled at her. "Good morning."

"Good morning," she said, her gaze going from his face to his summer-weight olive-green suit and back again. Then he realized he was doing the same thing to her, his gaze went from her professional blond chignon, along her facial features, down the lines of her royal-blue suit and back to her face again.

"You look great," he said, his voice almost a whisper because she took his breath away.

"Thanks," she said simply, ignoring his tone, apparently to get them out of the mood, as she pulled the gearshift into drive.

"No, I mean it. You look really great."

Her gaze skittered in his direction again. "So do you," she said.

"Oh, this old thing," he said, then tugged on the sleeve of his jacket, making her giggle and the sound of her laugh finally relaxed him.

He knew she was worried about their attraction, because he was too. He had never felt so comfortable, yet so on edge with a woman before. The edge he could satisfy by making love to her, but that was the problem. Bailey was a sweet, sincere woman and he didn't want to hurt her. The relationship he thought would be casual and fun was turning out to be something entirely different—something serious and rife with compelling emotions. And though most people would see that as a reason to pursue it, Tanner knew he couldn't; he didn't want to leave another Emmalee behind when he left for Florida.

Which was why he hadn't kissed her the night before and why he intended to keep this trip as pleasant and light as possible.

"So where are we going?" Bailey asked, breaking into Tanner's thoughts.

"We are actually, physically going to Smith Mansion, housed on Smith Plantation," he said, shifting on his seat so he could see her as he spoke. "It's an enormous white house, surrounded by forest. They raise horses. I hear it's fantastic."

"From all that information, I take it the Smiths are personal friends of one of your personal friends."

"Precisely," he said, not about to tell her the personal friend was a still-popular quarterback he met his one season in the pros. Because he hated to talk about his almost non-existent pro career. It had provided the cash for his business and that was good, but the injury itself set a chain reaction in motion that completely changed his life. He had adjusted but he didn't like to dwell on it.

"Must be nice," she said wistfully.

"What?"

"Being able to do things, being able to accomplish what you want just by making a phone call or two."

He shrugged. "It is."

"You take it for granted, you know."

"What?"

"The ability to get things done. You've had the gift so long I don't think you appreciate it anymore."

"Oh, I appreciate it. Especially this past week," he said, catching her gaze. "I felt very proud to be able to help find the money for the park. I never realized how much I cared. This town owns a little piece of my heart."

"I think everybody's hometown owns a piece of their heart," Bailey commented, then made the turn onto the entrance ramp for the interstate when Tanner indicated.

"Yeah, but this is different. All the years I was gone I never even missed Wilmore. Yet this week I was pulling out all the stops, asking for favors I had no right to ask."

Easing into traffic, Bailey said, "It sounds as if you love your hometown a lot more than you thought."

If he hadn't seen her fingers flex and unflex on the steering wheel as she made the casual observation, Tanner might not have realized that the conversation struck a nerve for her. She'd inadvertently confirmed his suspicions. She wanted him to like the town because she wanted him to stay in Wilmore. He knew he had set the stage for her to cultivate that notion of permanency in their relationship when he told her he wouldn't kiss her because he wanted something more. But he knew it had been a mistake. He had a very short flight of fancy about something he couldn't have, but that was all it was. Now he wished he hadn't voiced the thought out loud because he was somehow going to have to take it back. He wouldn't get involved with a woman who wanted him to stay any more than he would get involved with a woman he couldn't take with him.

Knowing there was no point to it, he didn't further pursue the topic of his loving Wilmore and instead changed the subject. Bailey either didn't notice or didn't mind, because the transfer took place without a pause and the easy conversation continued for the entire four-and-a-half-hour drive to Smith Mansion. The only problem was they were an hour and a half early for their lunch meeting.

Not knowing what else to do, they found a shopping mall. Thinking they were going inside to while away the hour with a cup of coffee, Tanner accompanied Bailey into the main entrance. When she paused at a woman's clothing store and gasped with delight at a black suit, he stopped, too.

"You like that?" he asked curiously because to him it was rather plain and humdrum.

"I love it."

"Don't you think it's a little on the simple side?" he asked, picking up the sleeve of the straight black suit. The skirt was too long to expose any of her great legs. The jacket was boxy. The suit was no fun for a man at all.

"Minimalist things are in vogue right now."

"Really?" he asked, peering at her. If long skirts and boxy coats were in style, men were in for a few long, disappointing years.

"Really."

Even mired in his own displeasure at the turn of fashion, Tanner noticed that she gave the garment one last longing glance, then rehung the jacket and turned in the direction of the mall concourse again.

"Let's go."

Puzzled, he didn't follow her. "You're not going to buy it?"

She stopped and smiled at him. "No."

"Why not?" He glanced at the suit, then at her. "You obviously love it."

"And I'm also in debt."

"Are your telling me your shop can't handle the monthly payments on your business loan?"

"My shop can handle the monthly payments just fine. But I want to get that loan paid off quickly because there are other things I need."

She turned and started to walk away again, and Tanner scrambled to catch up with her. "Like what?"

"Well, Flora Mae's black-and-white decor from the fifties actually came back in style this year. When I bought the place, I added chrome sinks and replaced the floor tiles and I was good to go. The place has a fresh, clean feeling about it."

He thought about her salon. The new chrome sinks and black-and-white floor tiles caused him to miss that the black chairs and white hood dryers were virtual antiques. Her shop was a combination of old blending with new, and though it had taken a keen eye to know what to keep and what to replace to get that kind of ambiance, he could see she had bigger, better plans.

"You would like to completely remodel, wouldn't you?"

She shrugged nonchalantly, but enthusiasm shone in her rich violet eyes. "I want the shop to be mine."

"A prototype," he suggested, hooking in to her ebullience. "Something you could model all your other shops after."

"That's the idea," she said, smiling.

Tanner stared at her. Just the simple lifting of her lips sent his heart rate into overdrive. Not for sexual reasons but because something about her smile made him happy. Something about her enthusiasm lit his own creative fires, and he realized that that was really why he was working so hard for their hometown. She inspired him, tapped into his need to work...made him feel alive again.

"I'm starting to see what you mean about my not appreciating how easily I get things done, but I think you have it backward."

She peered at him curiously. "What do you mean?"

"It isn't that I don't appreciate being able to accomplish things," he said, leading her into a fast food restaurant. "The truth is I miss what you're talking about, looking for answers, accepting and overcoming challenges." He paused long enough to order their coffee and pay for it. "That's why I like this revitalization committee so much. It isn't that I love the town. I miss the work."

"Could be," Bailey agreed, sliding into their booth. "So, is there anything I need to know before we meet Mrs. Smith?"

Her easy acceptance of his explanation relaxed Tanner. He chuckled and shook his head. "We're going into this blind. With only the knowledge that she's eccentric."

"We can handle eccentric," Bailey said confidently.

"I certainly hope so."

"Don't tell me you worry that you've lost some of the charm that got you where you are today?"

"Let's just say I'm worried that it's sleeping," Tanner answered truthfully, and realized he liked the fact that he could admit that to someone. He hadn't lost his money, his intelligence, his experience or his connections, but charm was a fickle, fickle trait. It really was a use-it-or-lose-it commodity. And the last two years of his business he had lost it. He had been running on empty, bored, tired. It was no wonder he sold out. No wonder he went looking for something new.

She patted his hand. "I don't think you have anything to worry about in the charm department."

Feeling the warmth of her palm on the back of his hand, he raised his eyes until he met her gaze. "I don't think you do, either."

She grinned foolishly. "We're going to wow this woman."

He grinned right back at her. "Yes we are," he agreed, recognizing that was another thing he liked about being with her on this project. He enjoyed being part of a team. Being half of a whole. He had the sense deep down inside that there wasn't anything he and Bailey couldn't do.

Warning bells went off in his brain. In the beginning all he had really wanted was a date with this woman. Four or five hours of her complete attention, culminating with a long, deep kiss, followed by three or four weeks of enjoying each other's company. If sex got involved that would be good. If it didn't he wouldn't be upset about it. But instead of their relationship following that uncomplicated plan, everything mushroomed. When he was at his parents' home, alone in his old room, he understood why that was wrong and he knew he had to get them on the right track again. When he was with her, all his reasoning went sailing out the window. He knew he could reach out and take tomorrow with this woman.

And that just plain scared him to death. He had already failed once in the forever-after department. He had failed.

Emma hadn't. She'd fought the good fight. But Tanner worked too much, left her alone too often, wanted things she didn't care to have. What made him think things would be any different with Bailey, a woman even more tied to his quiet hometown than his ex-wife had been?

Nothing. That's what. Bailey was definitely more ambitious than Emmalee had been. She was smarter, more talkative and even more interesting, but in a lot of ways, in the important ways, she was Emma all over again. A small-town girl who liked who she was and where she was. Not only had Tanner failed in convincing Emma to change, he had almost destroyed her in the process.

He wouldn't do that again.

"How do you do, Mrs. Smith," Bailey said, clasping the delicate hand the elderly woman had extended when they were introduced.

Mrs. Smith was a picture of the gentility of the Old South. With her light brown hair softly curled around her face and wearing a pink crepe dress that seemed to float around her, she didn't look as old as she was reported to be, but her manners and her mannerisms clearly indicated that she was from an era long gone.

She guided them to a formal dining room with a shiny oak table that stretched almost from one end of the long, ornate room to the other. Three place settings were arranged at the far end. Tanner politely seated Mrs. Smith, then took the chair across from Bailey. The old woman regaled them with stories of the South and the great state of Virginia as if she had survived the Civil War and fought half the battles herself, charming both Tanner and Bailey into the odd sense that somebody had misinformed them about this darling old woman.

But when they sat in the study after lunch to actually

discuss the grant, and Mrs. Smith got behind the huge cherry wood desk, everything changed in the blink of an eye.

"So, tell me," she said, motioning for Tanner and Bailey to take the green leather captain's chairs across from her desk. "Why does your puny little town think it deserves my money?"

Bailey knew her jaw dropped in surprise, but Tanner urbanely picked up the conversational ball. "We don't think we deserve your money. We don't even know what we have to do to go about applying for your money. We're here to discuss criteria. Why don't you tell us what kind of town you're looking to contribute to?"

"Hmm," she said, eyeing Tanner suspiciously. "I feel like you just turned the tables on me."

"Because I did," Tanner answered with his sweet, sexy smile.

"Hmm," she said again. "I usually don't lose control of a conversation so easily. You must be more experienced than I thought." She pulled a cigarette from a gold-plated case on her desk.

Tanner immediately rose to light it. "Don't let my looks fool you, Mrs. Smith. I may not appear old enough, but I not only started a company that I just sold for millions, but I also survived the loss of a pro football career and a failed marriage."

The sliver of emotion in his voice when he said the words *failed marriage* brought Bailey up short. He wasn't the kind of person anyone thought could be hurt, but apparently he had been. Before she jumped to the conclusion that Tanner was an innocent victim as Cora seemed to think, she acknowledged that splitting up a marriage was never an easy thing to do. Obviously, he had loved Emma at one time. Plus, there was the other matter he mentioned: his injury. No one gave two thoughts to the fact that he had lost his lifelong dream of playing pro football around the same time that his marriage dissolved. All anyone saw was that he picked himself up and started over again, becoming even more successful than he was the first time around. As if everything in life came easy to him. As if he never suffered or struggled.

"I know what it is to lose something you love." He glanced around the office. "This was your husband's room, right?"

Mrs. Smith nodded, then gave the den her own loving perusal. "He chose everything in here."

"He must have been a pretty smart cookie."

"A hellion on Wall Street in the sixties and seventies. The man had a Midas touch. I missed him intolerably for the first three years after he died. Took me forever to get on with the rest of my life."

Tanner nodded. "I don't doubt it."

"How about you?" she asked, motioning for Tanner to sit again with a wave of her cigarette. "What broke up your marriage?"

"Incompatibility."

Mrs. Smith batted her hand disapprovingly. "That's hogwash. Shorthand for saying you just didn't want to try."

"Actually, I did want to try. I thought I was trying. It was my ex-wife's decision to end the marriage. She asked me to leave, and I did. I moved to upstate New York."

With that admission, Bailey had to fight to keep from gaping at Tanner as a million questions popped into her head. From what he was saying, nothing about his divorce was as everyone assumed. Worse, he kept excluding the fact that all this happened around the time he was injured and lost his pro football career. If Emmalee had been the one to ask him to leave at the same time that he was struggling to come to terms with losing his life's dream, Tanner would have been devastated.

But he never said a word. Didn't mention that part of it.

"Ohh," Mrs. Smith said with a grimace. "I'd like to see the woman who thinks she's too good for you."

Tanner laughed. "She's a lovely woman whose second husband is a great guy and they have three fabulous kids. In fact, Artie is the mayor of Wilmore. He was going to come with me, but Bailey's really the committee's star player. You don't send in second string, when the star quarterback is available. Artie will be with us next time, though, if you would like."

"You're friends with your ex-wife's new husband?"

Tanner chuckled. "We've been divorced ten years. But more than that, I haven't been around town much over the past few years. I started a company when I moved away—"

"But I still live in Wilmore," Bailey said cutting in quickly, seeing an odd look come to Mrs. Smith's face. She sensed that Mrs. Smith wasn't digging for personal information out of curiosity but because she wanted evidence of the committee's community ties. Though Bailey would have loved to hear more of Tanner's history, the grant took precedence.

"Born and raised in Wilmore, in fact," Bailey continued. "We had a flood this spring—well, we have a flood of sorts every spring—but this one was bigger than usual and cleanup wasn't just pumping out basements and hosing down sidewalks and roads. We ended up having to rebuild and replace things. That was when we looked around and realized our town needed more than we had.

Parks aren't merely pretty places, they are places for kids to play and people to meet to talk, but we didn't really have one.'' She smiled. ''Frankly I think the flood was something like a wake-up call from God.''

That made Mrs. Smith chuckle. ''A wake up call from God?''

''Cleaning up after the flood brought the town together,'' Bailey explained.

''And brought me home,'' Tanner said, picking up when Bailey seemed to run out of steam. ''The stream that flooded runs along the back of my parents' property, so their land sustained major damage. I knew we needed erosion and sedimentation controls so I came home to see that they were properly installed. That's when I heard about the revitalization committee. Building parks is only a fraction of what this committee wants to do for our town.''

Mrs. Smith asked Bailey to explain what other projects she had in mind, and she listened with rapt attention. Finally, when it was nearly suppertime, Mrs. Smith sighed. ''It definitely sounds like you know what you want and you also seem determined to get it.'' She reached into her desk drawer and handed a packet of papers across the desk to Bailey. ''Here's the application. You'll be in front of my committee in two weeks, so don't drag your feet. Get this back to me as soon as possible.'' She looked from Tanner to Bailey, then back to Tanner again. ''Whom do I have my secretary call to set up the appointment?''

''Call me,'' Bailey said, extracting a business card from her purse.

Mrs. Smith gave the card a curious look, then she glanced up at Bailey. ''You're a beautician?''

''Yes, ma'am. I have my degree in business, but my

friend talked me into going to beauty school so that I could buy Flora Mae Houser's shop—''

"And you listened?" Mrs. Smith asked incredulously.

"Yes, I bought the shop and I run it, but I want to turn it into a franchise—"

"How interesting," Mrs. Smith said, interrupting Bailey coldly, deliberately cutting her off. The old woman's lips turned downward into a frown. Bailey watched Mrs. Smith's eyes lower until she was looking at the information packet she had given Bailey—as if she wished she could snatch it back.

Bailey wet her suddenly dry lips. "Really, I'm a competent person," she said, fearing that she had somehow undone all of Tanner's wonderful PR work. "Nowadays a woman needs a degree to run a beauty shop."

"A degree to shampoo hair and spread gossip? The next thing you'll be telling me is that it's required that you live in a trailer park," Mrs. Smith said, rising from her seat. "You'll be hearing from my secretary within the next two days about your appointment time with the grant committee," she said, leading them to the den door. "But don't get too excited about that," she added, eyeing Bailey disapprovingly. "I have final say."

With that she dismissed them. Bailey and Tanner thanked her, then walked up the long corridor to the front door, across the gray plank porch and down the steps to the sidewalk and Bailey's SUV. Bailey was nearly numb from the shock of hearing Mrs. Smith's parting comment. If Bailey correctly interpreted it, the town might lose this money because Bailey was a beautician.

"Give me your keys," Tanner said.

Suspecting he probably recognized she was a little too shocked to drive, Bailey complied. The blood was pumping through her veins. Her thoughts raced wildly. She had worked her butt off to get her degree, then her beautician's license and then to scrape together the down payment to buy the shop. She wasn't merely a beautician. She was a businesswoman. Yet Mrs. Smith thought she was trash.

That was the bottom line. Mrs. Smith thought she wasn't good enough because of her occupation. Never mind the degree. Never mind how hard she worked. Never mind that her business made enough money that she was working on ways to franchise. Never mind that she liked being a beautician. Just jump right to the stereotype.

Tanner calmly drove down the long tree-lined lane from Smith Mansion and pulled onto the highway. He drove a respectable distance, then maneuvered the car off the road, cut the engine, laid his head on the back of the seat and sighed. "Bailey, don't take any of that personally. We were warned she was odd. She proved it."

Still too numb to be angry, Bailey said, "Yes, she did."

"Come on," Tanner said around a groan. "Swear, scream, punch something. Her reaction was ridiculous. You have every right in the world to be furious."

"I'm not furious, I'm numb. All my life I watched Flora Mae Houser walk into church wearing the prettiest dresses. At one time or another every woman in Wilmore has worked for her. She was the heart and soul of the town. For God's sake, she earned enough money to put two daughters through law school and then buy a house in Florida. She retired sufficiently wealthy to spend the rest of her days playing golf and chasing old men. There's money to be made here. Lots of it. Enough to attract a few celebrity salon owners, who shall remain nameless. It shocks me that someone as supposedly intelligent as Mrs. Smith doesn't know that.''

"Some people can't see the forest for the trees," Tanner said soothingly. "A lot of people thought I was tough and rugged because I owned a trucking company—"

She peered at him. "Weren't you?"

"Well, yeah," he said, grimacing because he obviously recognized he wasn't proving his point. "But, Bailey, a lot of that was image because I was an ex-football star."

That was the thing that tipped her over the edge of the anger precipice. She slapped her dashboard. "Why does everything have to revolve around *image?*"

"Why do you care?" he shot back incredulously.

"I don't care," she said, but deep down inside she knew she did. Not because of Mrs. Smith, and in a sense not even because they could lose the woman's money, but because this was the bottom-line truth to her problems with Tanner. Deep down inside she didn't think she was good enough for him...or maybe not his kind of woman. And it hurt. It hurt that she couldn't even feel comfortable with the fact that she liked him.

And that, she supposed, was why she was so absolutely positive the man was going to break her heart.

"Well, you shouldn't care," Tanner said, turning to face her, but the second he caught her gaze, something happened. Bailey could feel it. It was almost as if he switched from being her friend, who was happy to be a help to her, into a completely different person.

Because he stayed quiet, she said, "When you look at me, what do you see?"

Tanner swallowed. "I'm not sure I know what you mean."

"Do you see me like Mrs. Smith does? A dreamer

from a small town who didn't know what to do with her degree so she got a beautician's license and pretended that someday she would open a franchise?''

"Now you're putting words in Mrs. Smith's mouth. And frankly I don't think she needed any help.''

Holding his gaze, Bailey said, "I'm not really putting words in her mouth. I just verbalized everything I saw in her eyes, and now I want to know if that's how you see me.''

"No," he said, but the word came out through a strangled whisper. "Most of the time I forget what you do for a living because other things preoccupy me.''

"Like what?''

"Ah, Bailey, let's not do this…''

"Like what?'' she demanded.

"Like the fact that you're strong, smart and determined.'' He paused and caught her gaze. "And that you have beautiful, strange eyes, skin that looks like it would melt under my palm and hair that seems to beg me to run my fingers through it every time I see you.''

"Two times you looked like you wanted to kiss me," Bailey pressed, refusing to let him get out of this, and wondering if she wasn't punishing him because she couldn't punish Mrs. Smith. "But you never did.''

"The situation is complicated—''

"I know that, Tanner, but a kiss is a kiss. It doesn't have to be complicated. We both know that. Yet every time it looks like you're going to kiss me you stop, as if there's something wrong with me.''

"There's nothing wrong with you," he said, groaning. Apparently determined to prove his words, he reached out and slid his hand along the back of her neck. He nudged her toward him at the same time that he leaned forward. Bailey only had time to register the look in his

eyes before he pressed his mouth to hers and her own
eyes drifted shut in ecstasy.

His mouth was full and firm, warmer and more delicious than she had expected. It closed over hers hungrily,
parting her lips effortlessly, shooting shafts of pleasure
through her. The kiss was long and deep and incredibly
sensual. And so was the way he held her. He didn't cling
to her or even try to maneuver her into more intimate
proximity. His one hand sprawled across her back as if
every inch of her skin were a delight to touch, as his
other hand fanned through her hair. He made her feel that
there wasn't a part of her he didn't want to possess, that
he needed her whole body, her entire person to feel complete in this kiss. Then he slowly pulled his mouth away
and slowly began to slide his hands away, too.

Opening her eyes, Bailey swallowed. She saw the curious way he was looking at her, but because of all the
sensations and thoughts clamoring around in her, she
didn't have time to wonder what he was thinking. No
one had ever kissed her so gently or so thoroughly before.
She couldn't stop her tongue from darting out to recall
the taste of him still clinging to his lips.

Tanner shifted away. "Okay," he said, his voice tight
and hoarse. "Now you know that I want to kiss you."

She swallowed. "Yeah."

"So what do you say we head for home?"

"Okay," she said, not quite sure what else to do now.
Not only was she feeling strange and wonderful, but he
was acting as oddly as she felt.

He drove her SUV onto the road again. "You're one
hell of a kisser," he said, more analytically than com-
plimentary.

"So are you," Bailey said, not only to return the praise
but because she finally understood why he was behaving

so peculiarly. The kiss had knocked him for as much of a loop as it had knocked her. He didn't know what to do about it any more than she did, and rather than hide that or play sophisticated-guy-well-accustomed-to-such-things, he wanted to meet it head-on, to talk about it, so it wouldn't get the chance to surprise them again.

"They teach you how to kiss like that in college?"

Bailey laughed. "No. And I'm not even going to venture to ask where *you* learned to kiss like that."

Tanner smiled. "Don't."

They had a normal, reasonably quiet dinner at a roadside restaurant, talking more about the grant and preparing the paperwork than anything personal. Because it was late and she could walk to her shop in the mornings, she suggested he take her SUV home and bring it back to town the next day. He agreed with that theory until he realized that driving her home meant that he would be accompanying her to her door.

He had talked about the kiss with quiet male confidence, but the truth was, inside he had been shaking. He had kissed hundreds of women and he had been sexually aroused before, but nothing had ever happened like what he had just experienced with Bailey. The arousal he could handle. Actually, he liked it. He liked that she made him feel like a man on fire with need. He could work with that. It was the other things that drew him up short, like the fact that he might never get to quench this need. He had feelings for her that were so confusingly different that he wouldn't risk making love to her. He had a sense that if he did, he wouldn't be able to leave her.

He was back to having thoughts of permanency and destiny, and after kissing her they didn't scare him as much as force him to admit he should get the hell away from her and stay away.

He stopped the SUV and pulled the keys from the ignition.

"You don't have to walk me up," she said.

"I'm not about to let you off at the bottom of your steps when anybody could be waiting on your porch for you."

"I let you off and make you walk up your steps," she said with a smile.

His eyes narrowed at her. "This is different."

"Turning chauvinist on me?"

"Not hardly," he said, opening his door and jumping out. "Wait until you see how much of the grant paperwork I make you do," he added when they reached her porch steps.

"Division of labor," she said approvingly. "I can handle my share. Besides, I want to knock that old bat's socks off with our business plan for the town."

"That's what I wanted to hear from you," he said. "I wanted to hear that you were going to make this application so perfect there would be no way she could turn us down."

By now they were at the top of her steps and at her front door. Shivery, wonderful, permanent feelings swept through him. Expecting them, he took the time to not only acknowledge them but identify them. Especially the one that felt "permanent." Because that was the one that triggered all the others, he decided that if he could just kiss her without getting the feeling that this relationship was meant to be permanent, he wouldn't have to stop seeing her.

He bent his head, pressed his mouth to hers and felt himself tumble into sweet softness so perfect he knew why the term *permanent* kept flashing in his brain. He wanted to keep this, to keep *her* forever. He wrapped his arms around her shoulders, pulling her close, feeling how very, very well they fit together. He deepened the kiss degree by degree, until he recognized she wasn't going to stop him.

So he stopped himself.

He didn't know what was going on here, but he did know that the second kiss confirmed what the first kiss had proven. Theirs could never be a simple, easy relationship, and if he didn't get away from her, one of them would get hurt.

He tapped his index finger against her lips. "Good night."

"Good night," she whispered back.

Though Tanner would have happily basked in the warm, airy feeling flowing through him, he walked away. He actually wished he could take back the past twenty-four hours and return them to where they'd been yesterday, but he knew he couldn't do that, either.

He'd promised himself the day he left Emma that he would never hurt anybody again and neither would he let himself get hurt again, so his only recourse was to leave.

# Chapter Six

"**S**he said what?"

Bailey didn't answer Cora right away. Instead, pretending the discussion didn't really bother her, she nonchalantly arranged her scissors and combs on her counter tray in anticipation of the arrival of the Friday-morning crowd. Regular customers had long-standing appointments for weekend hairstyles or cuts. Bailey had two perms scheduled. Cora had an entire wedding party for which she was doing trial-run hairdos to see how they would look with the headpiece chosen by the bride. Cindy would come in at noon and take the overflow customers. Today would be busy and Bailey didn't want to start it off negatively, but her emotions were in such turmoil she knew she needed to talk this out with her best friend.

"She said something insulting about living in a trailer and gave me the impression she thinks beauticians are low-life trash."

Cora stared at Bailey. "Does this woman live under a rock?"

"I don't know," Bailey answered with a short chuckle, feigning lightness she didn't feel. She had been insulted by Mrs. Smith, and those criticisms hurt, but she was even more confused about what happened with Tanner. Not that he had kissed her. They both knew that would happen sooner or later. The problem was that her reaction to him kissing her was stronger, deeper, more profound than she'd expected and it affected the way she felt about everything in her life.

"Doesn't she know that in a small town the beautician is like God? Not only does the shop owner make more money than nearly everybody else, but she knows all the good gossip."

"I think it's knowing the good gossip that probably ruined our reputations with the sainted Mrs. Smith."

"Well, she's just plain rude."

"No, she's rich, ill informed and happy in her ignorance."

"What did Tanner say?"

Bailey paused, not quite sure what to reveal, what to hold back, especially after the way he kissed her. His first kiss had knocked her socks off with its intensity, but the second was what started all the confusing feelings. Like the first, it aroused her and made her feel startlingly feminine, but his second kiss, the slower, deeper, longer kiss, the kiss he gave her of his own volition, also proved he cared a lot more about her than he was letting on. Up until that kiss, she thought he found her attractive, maybe even interesting, but she didn't realize he had genuine feelings for her.

Strangely enough, it was Mrs. Smith's behavior toward Bailey that inadvertently caused him to admit it. He didn't minimize the insults or pretend they hadn't happened. He also didn't think Bailey should just bounce back without giving them much attention. He thought she should scream or swear or punch something. He even suggested it. No matter how hard she pretended to be okay with what happened, Tanner saw she had been hurt, and it bothered him. Just like it bothered her that Emma had hurt him. She couldn't stand the thought of his being hurt. He couldn't stand the thought of her being insulted. They saw the pain or vulnerability in each other's lives that everybody else didn't see.

And that's what kept drawing her to Tanner and Tanner to her. They saw each other's real life. No one else in either of their worlds recognized they had troubles. Oh, everyone might have seen Bailey flounder for six months after she graduated from college, before she went to beauty school and got her life on track. But no one ever doubted she would get her life on track. They *expected* her to get her life on track. No one saw the pain behind the losses, the difficulty behind the decisions or the work it took to keep herself going some days. All anyone saw was the success. And from what she heard Tanner tell Mrs. Smith the day before, he suffered from the same problem. All anyone ever saw were his successes. No one saw his pain, his struggles.

Was it any wonder she and Tanner understood each other?

"He told me he wants me to make the grant application so perfect she won't be able to refuse," Bailey said, answering Cora's question.

"And you can do that!" Cora crowed triumphantly, making Bailey smile ruefully. Even Cora, her best friend, the woman with whom she went to grade school, the woman who was with her every darned day, didn't see the difficulty of her battles or the effort involved to win them.

"Yeah, I can do that," she agreed.

"Soooo," Cora Beth said, infusing the tiny word with meaning by dragging it out forever. "Did he kiss you?"

"Actually, Cora, I asked him to kiss me," Bailey said, deciding not to skirt the issue. Facing it head-on would force her to realize that she asked for this and now she had to deal with it.

"Oh, my gosh!" Cora gasped. "You didn't!"

"I did."

"And?"

"And, it was the best kiss I ever had."

"You had doubts?" Cora asked, giving Bailey an incredulous look.

Bailey laughed. "No, I didn't doubt that Tanner McConnell would kiss like a pro."

"So," Cora encouraged. "What else?"

"Well," Bailey said, then swallowed hard. What she was about to do right now was tantamount to revealing a confidence of Tanner's. Though he hadn't asked her to keep his secret, Bailey sensed he didn't realize how much of his life he had exposed when talking with Mrs. Smith. If he had, she genuinely believed he would have asked for her silence because none of this story had gotten around town before and she suspected that was because he or Emmalee didn't want it to. Since he hadn't asked her to keep this information to herself, her own protective instincts reared up and she did what she knew she had to do to guard Tanner.

"I'm only going to tell you the rest of this because I need your advice," she said softly, quietly, her eyes pleading with Cora to understand. "But you have to promise me that you won't breathe one syllable of this to anyone.''

"When June told us she had cancer and asked us not to say anything, didn't I keep my word?''

Bailey nodded.

"Okay, then,'' Cora said, serious now because Bailey was serious. "After twenty years of friendship I've proven I can be trusted. So spill it.''

"Tanner McConnell is not the guy we think he is.''

One of Cora's eyebrows rose. "You mean, Tanner McConnell is not the guy *you* think he is. I've been his defender all along.''

"I know that,'' Bailey said. "But what even you don't know,'' she said, looking Cora in the eye, "and this is the secret part…is that *he* didn't leave Emma. He also didn't refuse to take her with him when he went to New York. Apparently, the truth is she asked him to leave and he ended up in New York.''

Cora gasped. "He told you that?''

Bailey shook her head. "Not directly. That's why we need to keep it a secret. In sweet-talking Mrs. Smith, he let it slip that he had to recover from the fact that his wife didn't want him anymore.''

"That doesn't necessarily mean Emma asked him to leave. Anybody who gets divorced can be hurt—''

"No,'' Bailey said, shaking her head. "He said his wife asked him to leave. I would have remembered it regardless of how Mrs. Smith reacted. But the thing that etched it in my memory was that Mrs. Smith said something about being unable to imagine the woman who would think she was too good for him. Tanner laughed and defended Emma.''

"No kidding,'' Cora said with another gasp. She paused, combed her fingers through her hair, then added,

"I've always known there was more to this than met the eye, but I'm just having trouble assimilating that Emma dumped Tanner for Artie."

"I'm not sure that's how it happened."

"He didn't say?"

Bailey shook her head. "He didn't say."

"Wow, this puts a different spin on things."

"It's like he's this incredibly misunderstood nice guy, who also happens to be rich, successful and funny."

"Yeah," Cora agreed, but the one word came out on a dreamy sigh. "You are so lucky!"

"How can you say that?" Bailey asked dumbfoundedly. "The man is going to leave and I am going to be hurt because I'm really, really starting to like him."

"And what if he doesn't leave?" Cora asked suddenly. "Or what if being in a relationship with you makes him want to stay in Wilmore?"

Bailey stared at Cora. "That's a stretch."

"No, it isn't. But right now it's sort of irrelevant. You're only at the beginning of your relationship. You're at the stage where you're finding things out about each other. You're not supposed to be making lifetime commitments or decisions. This isn't the time to try to talk him into staying in Wilmore or even to pin him down about whether he would consider taking you with him if he goes. You're just supposed to enjoy whatever happens."

Bailey's mouth fell open in disbelief. "That's not how my life works! I can't live like there's no tomorrow."

"Bailey, get a grip," Cora said flippantly. "You can't control this the way you control everything else. Six months from now…six weeks from now…heck, six *days* from now, you might feel very, very different about how you want to spend the rest of your life. And, by the way, just like it isn't a stretch to think you might permanently entice Tanner home, it's also not a stretch to think *you* might want to leave with him, if and when the time comes.''

Bailey laughed. "With my business loan?" she asked sarcastically. "I'm tied to this town for the next thirty years.''

"And what if Tanner pays off your mortgage for you, then what?'' Cora asked tauntingly, but her mood changed and she sighed heavily. "Look, Bailey, you're only trying to plan this out because you don't want to get your heart broken like you did with that Dennis guy from college.''

"Yes and no,'' Bailey admitted because it was true. "Yes, because I don't want to get hurt again, and no, because the situations are entirely different. Dennis was a boy who used me. Probably because he didn't know any better. And I forgave myself because I was a young girl and I definitely didn't know any better. Tanner is a man,'' she said, and realized it was true. That was part of what was different in her experience with him. He wasn't a fumbling, inexperienced boy. He was a man. Technically he was the first *man* in her life. "And I'm a grown woman now, responsible for a lot of things. Not the least of which is this shop. I have to act responsibly.''

"Responsibly, yes, but not like a woman who is in prison,'' Cora groaned. "Bailey, for Pete's sake, you can't plan this out. It's something neither you nor Tanner can control. It's not even normal to try. Besides, you never know what the future holds. Like I said, he might like you enough to want to stay. Or you might grow to like him enough that you wouldn't mind leaving.''

Though Bailey tried not to acknowledge that the thought had even come to her mind, the second scenario had tremendous merit, and that was actually what troubled her. Everything in her life seemed to make sense until Mrs. Smith began poking holes in her plans. Who did she think she was to be scheming to franchise a small-town beauty salon? How did she possibly think she would bring that about? In the grand scheme of things beauticians weren't really that important, and it almost seemed that Bailey had talked herself into believing a dream that wasn't ever going to happen. If she had made a terrible mistake in buying this salon, if she was wasting her degree, leaving with Tanner would fix everything.

"What if I'm only suddenly interested in Tanner because I'm afraid I made a mess of my life?"

Cora turned from the curlers and combs she was arranging. "I'm not sure I follow."

"Look at this logically with me, Cora. Leaving with Tanner sounds like a quick, easy way to get out from under this shop," Bailey said, toying with the plug of her blow dryer. "What if I'm only attracted to him for his money like everybody else?"

Cora laughed. "I doubt that. But if you're worried, take a good hard look at the man the next time you're in the same room. You'll realize very quickly that even if he was dirt poor most women would be attracted to him."

Bailey sighed. "You're right," she said just as the bell sounded announcing Mrs. Jeffries. She smiled at Cora's first customer. "Hi, Mrs. Jeffries."

"Good morning, girls," Mrs. Jeffries said, producing a box of doughnuts from behind her back. "Look what I brought."

"Ohh! Doughnuts!" Cora cried, taking the box from Mrs. Jeffries and handing her a black cape. "You put this on and I'll go make a pot of coffee."

"My thought exactly," Mrs. Jeffries said with a laugh.

Bailey smiled, but as quickly as her lips lifted, they fell down again. The entertainment of her day was sugar and fat. Gossip. Fixing hair. She was so busy trying to come up with new hairstyles and improve her stylist skills that she knew her shop wasn't yet ready for the marketing or advertising she'd learned about in college. So those skills were languishing away, probably diminishing with every passing day. She didn't have time to follow the thoughts of the Federal Reserve on interest rates. So she had no clue about the state of the economy. She didn't read analysis from think tanks. Didn't plot strategies. She didn't even take in enough money or use enough supplies to need her computer software, and she couldn't remember the last time she even looked at her five-year plan.

Instead she ate doughnuts.

She tried to cheer herself up by reminding herself of the newly typed grant application she had in her briefcase, the one she had stayed up most of the night to complete. But in really thinking about it, she couldn't say her work on the revitalization committee was all that difficult. Some days it was nothing more than glorified secretarial work. Pulling together information and then typing it.

Mrs. Smith was right. Her life was cheap.

At the committee meeting that night, seated across the table from Bailey, Tanner stared at the long slender column of her neck exposed by her simple pale blue U-neck shirt and caressed by fat yellow curls that fell from her ponytail and bounced around her shoulders. He almost scrubbed his hand across his mouth in frustration. It didn't seem fair to be so attracted to someone he couldn't have. He hadn't had feelings like these since Emmalee, and though part of him wanted to bask in the joy of realizing he could be falling in love, the other part, the realist, kept screaming reminders of how terribly his first relationship had ended.

Not only had he been a horrible husband, not only had he hurt Emma to the point that she'd asked him to leave, but he'd never seen it. He hadn't recognized his bad behavior, hadn't realized he had been organizing her life, dragging her into situations and circumstances she didn't want to be pulled into. If he'd had one clue that he'd been hurting Emmalee, but mistreated her anyway, at least he could think that with Bailey he would change. But the truth was, he couldn't change what he didn't know he was doing. And that was the problem. He could easily fall into those patterns again with Bailey and not even know it.

After Artie was done opening the meeting, all eyes turned toward Bailey and she smiled, pulling the grant application out of her briefcase. Tanner wasn't surprised until he saw that the darned thing was not only completed, it was typed, and enough copies had been printed that everybody could have one.

"We'll go over my answers, one by one," Bailey said, passing out the sheets. "But I think you're going to see this is exactly what we want."

"I don't know," Artie said dubiously, glancing down at his copy. "Most of the committee didn't even know you'd gotten the grant application. So we haven't had time to consider what we want to say." He glanced at Bailey. "I think we should all take it home. Read it. Think about it."

Looking confident and in control of the situation, Bailey shook her head. "We don't have that much time,

Artie. The application has to be back as soon as possible
for Mrs. Smith's committee to consider it before a meeting that's scheduled for two weeks from now. Let's just
go over it tonight."

"I don't think so, Bailey," Doug piped in, sliding his
copy of the grant papers aside. "I know you're great with
this stuff, but there's more to these applications than digging up the answers and typing them in the blanks. Somebody serious has to look at this."

Tanner watched an odd series of emotions cross Bailey's face. Most of them he was sure revolved around
angry disbelief that apparently Doug didn't think she was
"serious." But rather than sputter with fury, she calmly
asked, "Are you saying I'm nothing but a secretary to
you guys?"

"Hell, no, Bailey!" Doug said with a gasp. "I know
you do a lot of work on these things." He shook his head
and smiled sheepishly. "But you're not very old. You
don't know the town like me and Artie and old Doc Jen-
nings."

"Yeah, Bailey," everyone at the table said, agreeing
with Doug.

Tanner glanced down at the answers she had given,
quickly reading through the first page and then looked
up again, catching her gaze.

"From what I just read, everything seems fine. But if
the guys want to take this home and get a better look at
it, the best thing to do is set a deadline," he said, smiling
encouragingly. "How about if we all agree to read this
tonight and tomorrow and have it back to Bailey by Sunday night's meeting?"

He saw Bailey's eyes register a sort of relief that his
deadline suggestion wouldn't allow the revitalization

committee to drag its feet, but there was something else reflected in her deep-purple orbs, too. Almost a sadness.

"Yeah. That would be great," she said. "Then I can revise it in the computer and send it out Monday by overnight mail."

"And we get it in, long before you meet Mrs. Smith's board, and they have plenty of time to review it," Artie said approvingly. "Works for me. So, unless there's any other business, I say we adjourn until Sunday night again. Bailey, that's okay with you, right?"

She smiled and nodded. Artie adjourned the meeting and Tanner asked Bailey for a ride home.

In the SUV he turned to her. "I get it."

"Get what?" she asked nonchalantly, but Tanner could sense she wasn't nearly as casual about the reaction of the committee to her grant application as she was pretending to be.

"You do just about everything for this committee," Tanner said. "Aside from Artie, I haven't seen anybody but you do anything except attend meetings. But when the chips were down tonight, they didn't trust you. It was insulting that they asked for the opportunity to privately check your answers. I think you have every right in the world to be really, really angry about it. So go ahead."

She peered at him. "I'm not angry about that. In a strange way I'm heartened by it. I'm always preaching that I want them to take a more active interest."

Tanner laughed. "Okay. We'll play it that way. It is good that they're taking an interest, but they could have been more tactful with what they said and how they said it."

"We're an informal committee, Tanner. And we're all equal, except for Artie. No one has to treat me with kid gloves."

He shook his head. "Bailey, this isn't a matter of treating somebody with kid gloves. Those guys insulted you. I saw the look on your face. And after the way Mrs. Smith treated you, you've got to be pretty miserable right now. I don't think it's healthy for you to pretend nothing happened or that it doesn't bother you."

"Oh, really?" she asked sarcastically.

"There, see? I heard that little bite of sarcasm. You're mad and you need to vent. You started to, after we left Mrs. Smith's mansion, but that got cut short," he said, trying to tiptoe around the fact that they'd stopped talking about Mrs. Smith because he kissed her. "I think you need to finish your ranting, to get this out and let it go. So why not do it with me so it will stay between the two of us and no one else will have to know."

"I do not need to rant."

"Of course you do. You're fuming inside. You need to let it out."

"All right. All right," she said, her fingers curling and uncurling on the steering wheel. "You want me to let it out? Here goes. I'm a twenty-five-year-old woman with a business degree, who bought a beauty salon and thinks she's someday going to be Paul Mitchell. But before I can put another shop anywhere outside of Wilmore, I know I have to establish myself as an artist, a hair artist— or find someone who is—so my salons can be unique and special. Since I know that could take more than a few years, I also know my business skills will go to hell in a handbasket unless I do something. But before I can panic about that, Wilmore has a flood, the town gets involved with all kinds of neat, interesting things like getting government loans and figuring out simple paybacks and finding money for things we need. And I think, hey, if I keep the committee going it will keep me on track professionally…but it didn't. It *didn't*," she said, her voice softening.

"How do you know that?" Tanner asked curiously.

"First of all it was fairly damned clear tonight that the committee considers a lot of the things I do nothing but secretarial work. And they're not alone. In trying to understand Mrs. Smith's reaction once she discovered my profession, I had actually come to that conclusion myself this morning. I'm a secretarial beautician. I'm wasting my degree."

"Bailey, you're taking Mrs. Smith's criticism to heart, and you shouldn't," Tanner said as she turned her SUV into the now-leveled lane of his parents' home.

"I have to!" she insisted. "Don't you see? Until you joined the committee, until I talked with Mrs. Smith, I felt like I was on the right track and everything seemed possible to me. Now I feel like a dreamer."

She stopped her vehicle in front of his parents' porch and turned to Tanner. "Because she made sense, Tanner. I'm a beautician with a business degree, who is not automatically, by magic, going to turn into a hair artist and become Paul Mitchell. Yet, if you listen to me talk, that's how I must sound." She paused and blew her breath out on a sigh. "I feel so stupid."

"You're not stupid and you're not a dreamer," Tanner insisted, but something she said kept repeating itself over and over in his head. *Until you joined the committee, until I talked with Mrs. Smith, I felt like I was on the right track and everything seemed possible to me.*

It was his greatest fear set to words. Just like with Emmalee he hadn't seen what he'd been doing, without intending to, he had interfered in Bailey's life. Maybe even changed it forever. By finding that foundation and introducing her to Mrs. Smith, he had pushed her into

things for which she wasn't yet ready. A few years down
the road, her committee might have unearthed Smith
Foundation on their own, and Bailey would probably
have been ready. It was his fault she felt defeated. It was
his fault she felt like giving up.

He shifted on the seat, caught her by the shoulders and
turned her to face him. "Listen to me, Bailey. Everybody
has a right to have a dream. No one deserves to have her
dream stolen by a bigoted rich woman so far out of touch
with reality that she probably doesn't even choose her
own breakfast. You can't give up because of one person's
opinion."

"You don't think I should quit?"

"No!" he said, emphasizing his statement by holding
her gaze. "I think you should keep going, keep doing
whatever it was you would have been doing if I hadn't
shown up."

His intentions must have seeped into the tone of his
voice, because she stared into his eyes for several seconds
then quietly asked, "Does this mean you're leaving?"

"Yes." He held her gaze. "As soon as I can. Not
because I don't like you," Tanner said, trying to make
sure she understood something he wasn't quite sure he
understood himself. "But because I *do* like you."

"Oh, that makes sense," she said, smiling miserably.

"It doesn't make a damned whit of sense," Tanner
said. He released the grip he had on her shoulders and
reached for the door handle. "But I'm about the worst
bet you could take for a lover or husband. I've already
dragged you into things that nearly ruined your confidence. That's what I do, Bailey. That's why my relationships fail. I'm so focused on myself and what I want that
I never see the other side of the story." He opened the
door. "So, I'm quitting while you're still ahead."

# Chapter Seven

On his way to the hardware store for his father, Tanner intended to stride by Bailey's salon without giving it as much as a passing consideration. The sky was blue. A summer breeze ruffled the trees on the mountain behind the town, exposing the undersides of the leaves to the morning sun and causing them to glisten like a wall of diamonds. Through several miracles of overnight mail, the parts for his Mercedes had arrived at the garage that morning, so technically he was free to go. Once he honored his commitment to attend the meeting with Mrs. Smith's board, he could be on his way. It was actually timely and appropriate that he told Bailey he was stepping out of her life.

Unfortunately, he just couldn't forget that last kiss.

He didn't even have to close his eyes to recall the softness of Bailey's lips pressed against his or the sensation of their tongues twining intimately. But if he did close his eyes and take one long breath, all the physical responses inspired by her warm mouth seemed to spiral through him. He felt hot and weak simultaneously, but more than that, the state, both the physical sensations and his emotional reactions to them felt *right*.

When he examined all the events that had brought them together he could almost believe they were supposed to meet. Yet, he knew that wasn't true. It couldn't be. He had already inadvertently thrown her into a situation for which she wasn't ready by introducing her to Mrs. Smith. If he were meant to be with her, his presence would enhance her life, not cause turmoil.

But he had caused turmoil. Lots of it. It hadn't been his intention to push her. He had been so involved with helping her help the town that he didn't even see he was doing it. But that was the problem. Just like he was so wrapped up in his own troubles that he didn't see the effect of his choices on Emmalee, he had been so wrapped up in this revitalization committee and getting a stupid date that he didn't realize he was pushing Bailey and threatening to destroy her dream. If that wasn't proof positive that he was wrong for her, Tanner didn't know what was.

No, he thought, and sighed heavily when he caught sight of Bailey's blond hair as she walked to the cash register in front of her shop window, chatting with a customer. They were not meant to be together.

Bailey peeked out the window and saw Tanner walking away. With his eyes hooded and his lips turned down in a serious frown, he looked like a man with the weight of the world on his shoulders. Bailey stopped talking with Mrs. Alshouse. Her hand curled tightly around the $4.25 worth of change she should have been handing across the counter and then froze above the open cash register drawer.

All she had to do was look at Tanner to remember what it felt like to kiss him. But it wasn't his warm, inviting mouth that came to mind first—though that did come to mind. It also wasn't the feeling of his strong arms closing around her, inching her nearer to his hard, muscled frame. No, what Bailey remembered, when she let her undisciplined mind drift, was the look on his face. She could see that kissing her shocked him in some way. She could also see from the smoky haze that darkened his eyes that their kiss affected him as much as it had her. But more than that she could see evidence of his recognizing everything she had been feeling since the day she met him: destiny, permanency, a knowledge that something special and important was happening or could happen between them.

But he wasn't going to let it. After only a day or two to think things through and without consulting her, he had decided to stay away from her. He said it was for the best since he was the worst bet she could take for a husband or lover because he never saw the other person's side of things. He even backed that up by accusing himself of throwing her together with Mrs. Smith before she was ready, but it seemed more to Bailey that he didn't want to try.

She understood he thought he was being gallant, but if she studied the situation closely, the real conclusion she drew was that he hadn't given the relationship much of a chance. After his confessions about Emmalee hurting him and how difficult it had been to lose his career, she would have thought he would be eager for a second chance at life and love, eager to explore this passion between them, no matter what obstacles they faced...

Yet, there he was. Walking away. She knew he wasn't a coward. She knew he wasn't weak. The only thing left for her to assume was that he was shallow. Gorgeously shallow.

Like Dennis.

"Bailey, honey," Mrs. Alshouse implored with a sigh. "My hand is getting tired. And you know how my arthritis is."

"Oh, gosh, I'm sorry!" Bailey apologized quickly, and poured the change into Mrs. Alshouse's hand before she closed the old woman's fingers around the coins and bills.

"I'll see you next Tuesday?" Mrs. Alshouse asked, then slid a rolled-up one-dollar bill into Bailey's hand for a tip.

"Next Tuesday is great," Bailey said. "But you know I can't take this. I own the shop now. You're not supposed to tip me."

"I know, dear, but I also know you had to take out a mortgage to buy this place. So, until you pay that off, a dollar here and a dollar there won't hurt the system, and it will do a lot of good on that loan."

Knowing it was pointless to argue, Bailey smiled. "Thanks."

"You're welcome, dear. I'll see you next Tuesday. Say hello to your mother for me."

"It's wing night at the bar tonight," Bailey said, calling to Mrs. Alshouse and stopping her when she reached the door. "Why don't you come? First dozen red hots are on me."

Mrs. Alshouse grinned. "No, the first dozen red hots would kill me. Besides, reruns of *ER* are on tonight. I'm still trying to figure out if Dr. Benton's a nice man or not."

"Yeah, me, too," Bailey said with a laugh and Mrs. Alshouse walked out of the shop.

Still smiling, following the old woman's progress

across the street, Bailey again caught sight of Tanner and her heart stopped. She found herself wishing that he were different, but skidded that wish to a screeching halt. She couldn't wish he were different. He was who he was. A man whose definition of a good relationship was flirting, kissing and having fun. If life with her couldn't be a lark, then he didn't want her. And truth be known, she didn't want him, either. She didn't want a man who wanted a perfect life, because she couldn't promise him one.

So she wouldn't wish that he were different. If she was wishing for anything, it was prosperity, a smooth path on her road to success. She may never give Vidal Sassoon a run for his money, but at least she could get within an arm's distance of Paul Mitchell. In fact, she thought, looking down at her calendar of appointments as Cindy and Cora happily cut the hair of chattering clients, she had Reggie O'Reily coming in in about fifteen minutes. What she should be doing was coming up with a way to convince the perky high school cheerleader to let Bailey try a new haircut on her. Free, of course. Because pretty, perky cheerleader Reggie would be a walking advertisement.

"You did what?"

Bailey sighed, looking across the window opening that separated the kitchen and the bar sections of her parents' tavern. Because it was only 5:45, the wing crowd hadn't really begun to arrive, and Bailey herself actually wasn't supposed to be here yet. But after her disaster with Reggie, and needing time with her parents not just for comfort but also to talk this through, Bailey had shifted her final haircut to Cindy—who was happy to take it—and had come to the quiet bar. A few ESPN patrons sat at the tables in the far corner of the room, nursing drinks as they absorbed the baseball game on TV, but otherwise the deliberately dark room was empty.

"I talked her into letting me give her this adorable pixie cut, and she flipped. She actually asked me to paste her hair back on again."

Bailey's parents laughed heartily. The short, stocky woman in her late forties, and the tall, bulky man in his early fifties were the picture of marital contentment. The Stephensons had opened the bar and restaurant together right after they got married. Joni Stephenson had taught her husband to cook out of necessity when their children began to arrive. Then, when the kids were raised and Bailey's mother came back to work at the bar, a sort of friendly competition developed. Joni had created the hot chicken wing recipe, and Bailey's father, Todd, came up with the secret sauce for pizza, but each was always trying to outdo the other. Sometimes they actually held cook-offs and let patrons eat free food and vote on whose offering was better. Because no one ever really knew which nights there would be free food, the house was usually packed by seven o'clock most weekdays.

Actually, that was what had given Bailey the idea to use a free haircut as an advertisement.

"Well, it backfired," her mother said, and Bailey realized she had said out loud at least part of what she had been grumbling in her head.

"You can say that again. Reggie hated it."

"Isn't she the little redhead who usually sits two rows up in church?" Todd asked as he twirled a pizza crust.

"The same," Bailey said with a sigh.

"Wasn't her hair already short?" he asked, confused.

"Short but unmanageable because of her natural curl. I gave her a cut that makes her hair manageable."

"Then why does she hate it?" Joni asked curiously.

"Well, it's considerably shorter than what she already had."

"Yikes, Bailey! What did you do? Shave her head?"

"No," Bailey mumbled.

"But damned close," her father speculated, obviously stifling a laugh. "Haven't we always told you to know your clientele?"

"Yes."

"So what part of 'know your clientele' did you not understand?"

Bailey stopped listening to her father's teasing reprimand because the bar door opened, bringing with it a beam of light from the parking lot. Walking in on that stream of light was Tanner McConnell.

From the corner of her eye she saw her mother nudge her father. "This will take her mind off the haircut."

"Not hardly," Bailey said. "My career is ruined. A handsome man hardly replaces a good career."

"Boy, where the heck did you get those screwed up priorities?" Bailey's father asked with a chuckle.

"I believe those were your words when you packed me off for college," she said, then turned and walked to the bar and Tanner who had just taken a bar stool.

"What would you like?" she asked quietly, avoiding his eyes, wishing the earth would just open up and swallow her. By now news of her failed haircut could be all over town. Even older, macho rich guys would have heard about it.

Waiting for his order, she ran a rag down the smooth wooden surface between her and Tanner, pretending to be inordinately busy, but Tanner didn't answer her for so long Bailey was forced to look up at him. When their eyes met, her knees nearly buckled. Dressed in an open-necked shirt and jeans with his hair neatly combed and looking at her as if she were dessert and he was hungry, Tanner McConnell sent her heart rate into overdrive.

"I heard about your trouble."

The pitter-pattering of Bailey's heart ceased. "Well, it's official. If older men are in the loop on this, I might as well close up shop."

He gave her a pained look. "Older men?" he asked incredulously.

"You know what I mean." She ran the rag down the bar again. When he still didn't give her a drink order, she said, "Come on, Tanner, what do you want?"

"Just give me a draft."

He named the brand, and Bailey turned away to face the tap and pour his beer. Tanner ran his hand along the back of his neck, not quite sure what he was doing here. All he remembered was feeling that Bailey would be upset and it was his duty or responsibility or something to talk her through this, and no matter how much he tried to argue himself out of it, he couldn't. Even reminding himself that he had interfered enough already didn't stop the urge to run to her aid.

But she not only didn't want his help, she also looked ridiculously cute in jeans and a belly-teaser T-shirt. She'd tied her long yellow hair into a swaying ponytail that danced around her every time she moved. Tempting him, teasing him, almost taunting him with something he couldn't have.

She handed him his beer. He fished into his pocket for a dollar, but she said, "Why don't you just run a tab? If you're staying for wings, it's easier that way."

"Oh, is it wing night?" he asked, unexpectedly happy to have stumbled in on Wilmore's big event of the week. Friday nights were official date nights at the bar, and her parents sometimes had a band on Saturday nights but nothing beat wing night.

"Do your parents still do that thing where they make ridiculous amounts of pizza or wings or spicy fries, give them out for free and then have customers vote on who's the better cook?"

Tanner watched Bailey struggle with a grin that she never did control. "Two weeks ago they made tacos. My mother even went so far as to make her own shells. My father made nuclear strength hot sauce. I thought George Peterson was going to end up in the hospital."

As she said the last, the bar door opened and the O'Donnell family entered, obviously about to make wings and fries their Tuesday-night supper. Bailey automatically reached for a small, multipocketed apron. She tied it around her waist, and Tanner held his breath. When he realized the apron more or less anchored itself on the waistband of her jeans and stayed there, leaving that lovely strip of smooth white tummy exposed, he let his breath out on a loud whoosh. Luckily, Bailey was well on her way to the O'Donnell table by then.

He rubbed his hand across the back of his neck again, chastising himself for being stupid. He could have any woman in the world he wanted, so why was he hanging around the one woman he had chosen to sacrifice on the altar of good behavior? His near obsession not only didn't make sense, it was also starting to annoy him.

The door opened again and two other families arrived. Because Bailey hadn't yet finished taking the O'Donnells' orders, Tanner rose from his seat at the bar, reached around to the shelves on the other side and grabbed a handful of menus. He passed Bailey on his way to distributing them.

Tucking her pencil behind her ear, she said, "You don't have to do that."

He smiled. "I know. It's not a big deal. I'll give these out. You take the O'Donnells' order to your parents. And by the time you get back, the Fishers and Johnsons will probably be ready to order."

"Okay," she said, breathing a sigh of relief before she headed off to the kitchen again.

"Hey, Tanner," Mark Fisher said, as he seated his elementary-school-aged boys around the table. "You slumming tonight?"

"Helping out," Tanner said, distributing the menus.

"We don't need these," Mark's wife, Jennifer, said. "We want three dozen mild wings in a basket," she said, deferring to the sensibilities of her children, "and a basket of fries and cola for each of us."

"Okay," Tanner said, regathering the menus he had just distributed. He turned to the Johnsons, who had taken the table beside the Fishers, and gave the menus to them before walking to the kitchen.

"The Fishers want three dozen mild wings, a basket of fries and some cola. How do I do this?"

"Write the order on one of those slips," Todd Stephenson replied as if having a guest waiter wasn't an unusual thing in this family-owned, hometown bar that served as a restaurant on most weeknights. "That's for the IRS," he added, giving Tanner a significant look and causing Tanner to laugh. "Then hang it on that turntable. Mother and I will make the food. You get the drinks, napkins and silver and set up the customers' table. We'll hit that bell," he said, pointing at the silver bell with his chin, "when your food is ready."

"Good enough," Tanner said, grabbing one of the pale green order tablets.

"You might want to get a pocket apron," Joni suggested, speedily dipping wings into an egg mixture before dropping them in ultrafine, powdery crumbs.

"I don't need an apron," Tanner said, hoping he didn't sound like a macho idiot. "I'm not worried about spilling anything."

"Well, you're actually going to want it for your order book and straws," Joni said, continuing to work like a woman possessed. "But if you think you can handle carrying everything, that's fine. We never argue with volunteer waiters."

Pleased that the senior Stephensons seemed to take his help in stride, Tanner was surprised when Bailey greeted him with thinly veiled hostility. "You don't have to do this."

"I know, but I want to," Tanner said, reaching for fountain glasses to pour cola from the tap. "I can't remember the last time I did anything so sane and yet somehow so frivolous."

"I don't appreciate being a lark for you," Bailey snapped, placing the glass of beer and three sodas she had just drawn onto a tray. "Everything might be fun and games to you, Tanner, but some of us are struggling to have lives here. Your popping in and helping when you feel like it, and disappearing when you don't, demeans us. Not just here but on the revitalization committee, too."

Flabbergasted, Tanner watched Bailey storm away, her ponytail swinging behind her, and his blood began to boil. Because he knew she appreciated his efforts on the revitalization committee, it took him a few seconds before he ascertained what was really wrong. She was angry about him stopping their relationship before it really got started. But he didn't want to stop it any more than she

wanted him to. Unfortunately, it was for her own good.
And she knew that. He had told her that. He made himself abundantly clear. So he didn't have a clue why a
levelheaded decision that saved both of them a lot of pain
would suddenly infuriate her.

But, because he had been staring at her as she worked,
he did notice that having an apron for straws made her
job easier, and he defiantly grabbed one of the aprons
from the top shelf beneath the bar.

"The way I see this, we'll alternate tables," he said
as he passed her on his way to serve the beverages to the
Fishers. "That means the next customer who comes in is
mine."

"Fine," Bailey said, sliding around him.

Tanner noticed the oddest thing. The tables were so
close together that to pass him Bailey had to suck in her
breath or brush against him, and he realized that was
another thing bugging her. They would be in each other's
company for the next few hours—each other's intimate
company because of close quarters—and she didn't like
it.

It amused him that her sexual attraction to him made
her huffy, but before he could even form a halfway-
decent chuckle about that, the reminder that she was sexually attracted to him poured through him as delicious
warmth. He always knew this wasn't a one-sided attraction, but he'd never had such clear confirmation before
and he couldn't help the burst of happiness to his ego.

And then he remembered that she wouldn't merely be
bumping into him and having reactions to him, he would
also be sliding past her, reaching around her, brushing up
against her, and a tingle of arousal rippled through him.
That was when he knew he had to get a hold of himself.
He wasn't allowed to have this fantasy any more than he

was allowed to let himself misbehave in front of an entire town.

He drew in a long breath and turned around just in time to see two couples come giggling into the bar. His turn. He patted his apron pocket to make sure he had an order pad and rounded the bar just as Bailey was returning to get drinks. Careful not to touch her, he made his way around her and headed in the direction of his table.

The bar door opened and three men came strolling in and ambled up to the bar. Tanner stopped, confused, but Bailey took their arrival in stride. She quickly asked for drink orders and then listened to their wing choices as she poured their drafts. She made waitressing look easy, while Tanner struggled to get his order pad out of his apron pocket and his new customers happily shouted their selections without the benefit of the menu.

As he scribbled, two more groups arrived. One group sat at a table near the jukebox and immediately began inserting coins, adding music to the existing cacophony of conversation, laughter and movement. As the first group made their selections at the jukebox, Bailey took orders from the second group, which had seated itself in the empty table by the bar. Walking to the tap for drinks, Bailey hooked her order sheet on the rotating holder for her parents. Then she grabbed glasses, poured drinks, served them and was on her way to the now sitting jukebox people before Tanner had finished taking his order, submitting his slip and pouring his drinks.

"I get the next table," he mumbled because now it was starting to feel like a competition. She didn't want him around because she was attracted to him, and apparently she had decided to get rid of him by making him feel slow and stupid.

Well, he wasn't about to feel slow and stupid. He was

new to waiting on tables, but he wasn't stupid and he certainly wasn't *slow*. Suddenly reminded about her comment that even the "older" men had heard about her disastrous haircut, Tanner's eyes narrowed in consternation. He wasn't that old. He wasn't even really old enough to be categorized as one of the town's "older" men. And she knew it. She'd only said that to get his goat. Well, she wasn't getting his goat. He might not be able to beat her at this game, but he could certainly keep up with her.

From there on everything began to happen in a blur. He took orders, poured fountain drinks and drafts, distributed menus, napkins and straws and served food as if he had been born to do it. Because both he and Bailey were working overtime to avoid touching each other, even accidentally, both had become adroit at shifting and turning, pivoting and spinning and just plain sucking in their breath to diminish the size of their torsos. Their movements almost reminded him of a choreographed dance, which had the unfortunate effect of making the whole thing seem doubly sensual, then Reggie O'Reily walked into the bar, her parents directly behind her.

"I'll get them," Tanner said, if only because he noticed the way Bailey seemed to freeze in place when she saw the three people come in from the dimming outside light.

As if he had suggested something evil and vile, Bailey turned on him. "I'll get them," she snapped, grabbing menus.

"Whoa, whoa," he said, pressing his hand on top of hers, preventing her from taking the plastic-coated sheets. "This isn't really a good idea for you."

"I think it's a peachy idea."

He shook his head. "No, it isn't. Because one bad PR

move in a town this size could kill you. Think this through, Bailey, you need to back off."

"Oh, really, Mr. Hotshot Business Owner? And what if they've come in here to see me? Everybody knows I work wing nights."

"And what if they actually came for wings," Tanner countered, nose to nose with her.

"All right, you two. Take it outside," Bailey's mother called through the window. "It's about time for you guys to have a break, anyway. Todd and I will serve the food that's up."

"No, we'll stop fighting," Bailey mumbled, straightening her apron.

"Yes, Mrs. Stephenson," Tanner said contritely. "We'll stop fighting."

"It's too late for promises," Joni replied with a chuckle. "I said take a break, so take a break."

"Fine," Bailey said, slicing one of her apron strings through the other with a quick yank. She tossed it on the bar and began marching to an almost hidden side door. When she reached it, she punched on the release handle and the thing sprung open, ushering her to the alley behind the bar.

Not quite sure what else to do, Tanner followed her. The second the door closed behind him, Bailey spun on him.

"Stop lecturing me."

He stared at her. The one thing he had vowed he would never ever again do was interfere. So he knew he hadn't lectured her. What he had done was offer obvious, normal advice to a friend. "What the hell are you talking about?"

"You think you know everything!" She paused, drew a quick, ragged breath and said, "You probably do know everything, but that doesn't mean I need the value of your expertise every damned time you see me screw up.''

Because he listened closely to everything she was saying, Tanner thought he heard the real genesis of her trouble, and he stared at her. "You can't stand that I've seen you fail?"

"I don't care that you've seen me fail. For Pete's sake, the entire town knows I failed at that stupid haircut. I should have known better," she said, and began to pace.

"Well, if you're not mad at me because I know about your haircut, that only leaves one other reason you can't stand to be around me."

She faced him. "Oh, really?"

"Yeah."

"And what would this amazing reason be?" she asked.

"You want to sleep with me."

He said it with his most charming grin, deliberately baiting her, because she looked so tightly coiled he was afraid she would explode. Worse, he was afraid she would say something she would regret back in that bar. Not that he thought she would lose her temper with Reggie's parents. On the contrary, he was afraid she would offer them half the shop to placate them.

"You are so egotistical I can't even think straight."

"Then deny it," he said, taking the three steps that separated them in slow, cautious movements.

"Easily."

"Say the words," he insisted, settling his hands on her shoulders, partly so that she couldn't get away and partly to prove his point. The two of them couldn't even touch accidentally without wanting to spontaneously combust.

"I don't want to sleep with you," she said, but the last words came out on a feminine quaver.

"I thought so," he said, then he laughed. "We're really a pair. I'm trying to do the right thing and stay the hell away from you, and you're trying to ignore me and we're failing miserably."

"Yeah, well at least you're only failing at avoiding me. I'm just plain failing."

"No, you're not. You blew one haircut. Did you ever stop to consider that you messed up because you're having trouble focusing?"

That got her thinking. "No."

"Okay, then recognize that you had a difficult encounter with Mrs. Smith—and it temporarily short-circuited your better judgment. Forgive yourself and move on."

"I can't," she said, sounding furious with herself. "I don't have the time or the money to waste on mistakes."

"Bailey, you better get used to making mistakes because a new business is riddled with them. Even though you inherited existing clientele, you're still new to them. You're going to have good days and you're going to have bad days. Count yourself lucky to have gotten one of your bad days out of the way."

He sounded so sweet and so sincere that Bailey only stared at him, wondering what the hell she was going to do when he left town, and why he thought he couldn't see anybody else's side of things when he always seemed to be around when *she* needed him. There was no reason for him to run from their relationship. If he wanted to, he had the insight to make it work, but something held him back and it made him as sad as it made her.

Because his hands were already on her shoulders, she only had to step forward to walk into his embrace. Sliding her hands along the small of his back, she hooked them together around his waist and pressed her cheek to his chest.

"Oh, Tanner, her hair looked wonderful! Why did she have to cry?"

"I don't know, Bailey," Tanner said, hugging her fiercely. "She's just a kid. Maybe it scared her."

"I'm sure it did," Bailey said, breathing in the scent of him as she absorbed his strength from his arms around her. "Which makes it even more obvious that I should have known better!"

"How? You're starting a new business," Tanner said, then he put his hands on her shoulders and set her away from him again so he could look in her eyes. "You're taking risks. That's what new businesses are all about. You're trying to prove yourself just different enough from the competition to be better. In any business you're riding a fine line. Trying to prove your price is lower, though your service is just as good, or your product is better so you deserve a higher price. In your case it's doubly risky because you're dealing with some variables you can't control. One of them is fashion. The other is the reaction of your client. And believe me," he said, smiling into her eyes, "women can be brutal on your ego."

Bailey couldn't help it, she laughed.

"Feeling better now?" he asked, pulling her into his arms again and rubbing his chin across the top of her head.

Bailey could have stayed just where she was for the rest of her life, but she knew there was work to do. She knew she had to face Reggie and her parents sometime, and she also knew Tanner was leaving. He liked her, he wanted her, but something stopped him from committing to a real relationship with her, and though she would love to argue him out of his decision, she couldn't. This choice had to be his. She took a pace back, out of his arms.

"We really should go in now."

"Do you think you can serve food without threatening to start World War III with me?"

"Hey, if I can go in there and talk with Reggie and her parents, handling you is small potatoes."

"Ouch," he said, grabbing his heart. "You are determined to kill me."

"Nah, keep you in your place, maybe, but not kill you," she said, laughing as she headed for the door again because she wanted him to see that she was fine without him. She had to be. She had a business to run. She had debts. She had employees who depended on her. Not only did she refuse to give him a guilt trip over his not being able to have a relationship with her, but also she really did have to get on with the rest of her life.

Even before Tanner was fully in the building, Bailey grabbed an order pad and headed for Reggie's table. At first Tanner almost panicked, but when he saw the happy greeting Bailey got, he stopped dead in his tracks. He didn't have to hear the conversation to understand that rather than being upset about her hair, Reggie now appeared thrilled with it. She combed her fingers through her short tresses, changing the shape ever so slightly and instantly creating a whole new look for herself.

Crossing his arms on his chest, Tanner observed the animated conversation between Reggie's mother and the now-happy Bailey, and he suppressed the urge to shake his head in wonder. Starting a trucking company was beginning to look like a piece of cake compared to running a beauty salon. He would take six angry, burly men any day of the week over one teenager.

He turned to retrieve his apron from the bar where he had tossed it, and as he did he saw Emmalee, Artie and their three children sitting at a table in the far corner of

the room. Emma caught sight of him and waved him over
to her table.

Tanner froze. He had the oddest sensation that after
ten years of almost no communication suddenly Emma
wanted to be his best friend, or to at least be a part of
his social circle, and he remembered why he was damned
glad to be moving to Florida. He didn't want to make
amends with her, not now, not ever. It wasn't just the
fact that she had hurt him, it was the way she had hurt
him. The insulting things she had said. The story that he
didn't want to take her with him when he moved to New
York—which evolved through gossip when neither of
them revealed much about their divorce—saved his ego,
but he was starting to realize that Emma might be the
lucky one. Everybody still thought she was a princess,
the town sweetheart, somebody above insults and petti-
ness, but she hadn't been that day. She also hadn't taken
his injuries or his confusion into consideration when she
bombarded him with accusations.

And she also hadn't given him a second chance. A
chance to make amends. To fix the marriage he'd so desperately wanted to keep.

He glanced at the apron he had almost retrieved and
shook his head slightly, disregarding that idea. She would
love that. She would love to see him wearing that apron,
taking orders from customers, playing waiter. And one
thing Tanner had vowed in his life was that he would
never do anything that Emma wanted him to do again.

He stepped back, away from the apron, and glanced
around. Bailey was fine. Actually, if the glowing look on
her face was anything to go by, she was better than fine.
The dinner crowd was slowing, and all Bailey would
have to handle soon would be the bar patrons. He had a
satisfied sense that he had accomplished whatever it was

fate had wanted him to do when he came into this bar tonight. And he could leave. She didn't need him anymore.

But a shaft of disappointment went through him when he realized that, because it was true. She didn't need him. No matter how much he wanted to think fate was telling him Bailey Stephenson needed him in her life, he knew it wasn't true. She didn't need him. He could go.

Quietly, unobtrusively, he slid out the back door.

# Chapter Eight

As Bailey drove to the McConnell residence to pick up Tanner for their meeting with Mrs. Smith's board of directors, she didn't notice the splash of color against the mountain-hewn horizon as the sun burst forth, or the awakening wildlife in the forest along the way. She couldn't stop thinking about the fact that this was something like her moment of truth. Or maybe her time of decision. Considering the almost-fiasco with Reggie's hair, if she couldn't convince Mrs. Smith's hopefully sane board of directors that her desperate little town deserved a grant for a park—one measly park—then maybe she didn't have the stuff to create a prototype salon that could be turned into a franchise.

And she had to face that.

When she pulled up beside the porch steps, Tanner was nowhere around. She saw light in the square panes of glass in the front door, but it was dim, as if far away, raising Bailey's suspicions that Tanner could have forgotten about their meeting and might not be ready.

She hadn't missed the way he'd disappeared from her parents' bar, and knew he had done that because he didn't want his few minutes of consolation to give her the wrong impression. He hadn't changed his mind. There could be nothing between them but friendship—and that was another thing she just had to face—but she didn't think he had deserted the revitalization committee, too. He promised to keep his commitment, and she knew he would.

She jumped out of her SUV and sprinted up the steps and across the porch. Before she got a chance to knock, Tanner's mother answered the front door.

"Well, hello, Bailey, dear."

"Hello, Mrs. McConnell," Bailey said, as she appraised Tanner's mother's hair. "Looks like that perm we gave you is holding up nicely."

"That's because I wear my hair in a bun a lot and I don't put too much strain on the curls," she said, opening the door wider so Bailey could enter. "Tanner's still eating breakfast. French toast. Want some?"

"No," Bailey answered automatically, then her nose caught the scent of the food and she grimaced. "Yes. I'm starving, and I would love some."

"Good." Doris smiled as she led Bailey into the family's bright and shiny kitchen. From the new look of the avocado-and-almond appliances and countertops, and the brilliant green and white ceramic tile floor, Tanner didn't merely spoil himself; he was a generous benefactor to his parents.

Right now he sat at the kitchen table, reading the morning paper. Wearing a cream-colored shirt and paisley tie, with his suit jacket draped over the back of an empty chair, he looked professional and intelligent. Just old enough to have the experience to be successful, but not so old as to be out of her reach. He was the perfect combination of youth and seasoning. He was everything Bailey had ever wanted in a man, yet he wasn't the man for her or he wouldn't be so determined to stay away from her. He kept saying that he was trying to do the right thing, but despite his obvious generosity with his parents, Bailey didn't think the decision to stay away from her was purely benevolent, made solely to protect her. Emma had hurt him. He admitted it to Mrs. Smith, but he had never admitted it to Bailey or anybody in Wilmore, so she didn't feel free to talk with him about it. Because he wouldn't confide it, she couldn't even argue that she was different from Emma and wouldn't ever hurt him.

"Good morning, Bailey," Tanner said, closing the paper the second he glanced up and saw her. "Sorry I'm late."

"Don't be sorry," Bailey said, taking a seat at the table. "Because you were slow, I'm getting French toast, too."

"Good," Tanner said, setting the newspaper aside. "What's the game plan for today?"

"You don't have one?" Bailey asked incredulously.

He shook his head. "I'll support you in any way I can, but I told you I'm no longer taking the lead. This is your show, Bailey, your town. I'm only visiting."

When he said the last, Bailey remembered that this had been the issue that stood between them all along. He wasn't staying in Wilmore. Knowing what she did now, she couldn't help but believe that this had more to do with Emmalee than Tanner's fervent wish to own a charter fishing boat business in Florida. And she wondered, really wondered, what the heck had happened between him and his ex-wife that could be so awful he wouldn't even want to be in the same town with her anymore.

"Well, lucky for me, then," Bailey said, continuing the conversation, "that I spent the past week and a half coming up with a presentation. I have my portable computer in the car and I created a series of visual aids that demonstrate my points. I called Mrs. Smith's secretary to be sure they could accommodate my system with their screen, since my computer can serve as the projector of sorts, and Amanda assured me they can."

"You're on a first-name basis with Mrs. Smith's secretary?" Tanner asked with a grin.

"Hey, you make your friends and allies where you can. Given Mrs. Smith's attitude," she said as Tanner's mother served her a plate of piping hot French toast, "I thought it best to have at least one person on my side going in."

"Nice strategy," Tanner agreed, handing her the maple syrup.

"I thought so," Bailey said.

Doris took a seat at the round table between Tanner and Bailey. "So, Bailey," she said, "I heard about Reggie's haircut."

Tanner almost dropped his fork, wondering what the heck would have possessed his usually diplomatic mother to bring up such a sensitive subject.

But Bailey smiled. "I can't believe I got so much mileage out of one hairstyle."

"Reggie's a cheerleader, everybody notices her. Which means everybody was noticing that nifty little hairdo you gave her."

Tanner looked from Bailey to his mother and back to Bailey again. "So it's a nifty little hairdo now?" he said, but he remembered at Bailey's parent's bar he had seen that Reggie had changed her mind about the new style.

"It was a nifty little hairdo ten minutes after she left the shop and her friends got a look at it. Unfortunately, most adults only saw her running from the salon crying. That's how the rumor got started."

"Right," Tanner said, glad the world of beauty salons could remain completely foreign to him because it was just too darned capricious. He rose from his seat. "I'm going to go upstairs to finish getting ready. I'll be down in about ten minutes."

"I'll be done by then," Bailey assured him. "I don't plan on eating all of this," she said, laughing as she pointed at the tall stack of French toast on the plate Doris had given her.

"Bailey, you should eat more!" his mother said, scolding her with a sigh. "You're too thin."

"I don't think so," Tanner said, walking out of the kitchen. He jogged up the steps to his bedroom, found his cuff links, brushed his teeth and ran back downstairs again. When he reached the kitchen, he couldn't help but note that his mother was leaning in, listening with rapt attention to everything Bailey was saying.

"Sorry to break this up," he said, "but we've got to get going."

"Yes, we do," Bailey agreed, rising. "Thanks for the French toast, Mrs. McConnell."

"Oh, you can call me Doris," Tanner's mother said, and Tanner cast her a skeptical look. She didn't let anybody under the age of fifty call her Doris.

He wondered if he should worry that his mother might play matchmaker, but remembered there was nothing to be concerned about. His car was fixed, the erosion and sedimentation controls were almost completed, and even his business with the revitalization committee was coming to an end, so he would be leaving soon.

The thought gave him an unwanted pang of sadness, but he ruthlessly squelched it, switching his focus from what he was losing to what he was gaining. How could a man possibly be sad over the opportunity to move to a warmer climate and start a charter fishing business? He would have to be nuts.

The meeting with Smith Foundation's board was held in the conference room of the Charlottesville offices for the corporation in which Mrs. Smith's family still maintained controlling interest.

A smiling Amanda led Bailey and Tanner into a long, thin room furnished with an ornate cherry wood conference table surrounded by sixteen thickly padded celery-colored chairs. Beige vertical blinds were closed to keep out the early-afternoon sun. A matching cherry wood credenza held a silver water pitcher and coffeepot, as well as delicate green-and-peach floral china cups and saucers.

"Ms. Stephenson, Mr. McConnell," Mrs. Smith said, rising from her seat.

All the board members in attendance rose with her. Bailey quickly noted that the group was a jumbled combination of men and women, young and old. There was no median age or gender majority at the table. She didn't know if that was good or bad. But she did recognize that fourteen of the sixteen chairs were filled, indicating that Mrs. Smith had a large family and Bailey had a lot of people she had to convince.

She and Tanner walked to the empty seats, which were side by side, positioned in the middle of the table to ensure that everyone could see and hear them. Tanner pulled out her chair for her, but Bailey shook her head.

"Mrs. Smith," she said, "I mentioned to Amanda that I had some overheads…"

"Yes, dear, the screen pulls down from the ceiling above the credenza." She paused and glanced at one of the male board members. "Harvey, would you get that?"

Bailey took a few minutes to quickly set up her computer and organize herself. When she was ready, she drew a quiet breath and smiled at Mrs. Smith.

"Ready, dear?" the old woman asked condescendingly, as if needing time to assemble her computer somehow made her stupid.

Bailey felt her blood began to heat with anger, but she controlled herself by telling herself to look at this as the test that she knew it was. If she couldn't handle getting a grant for a park from a foundation established to give grants for parks, then her plans for building a beauty empire were not only out of her reach, they were foolish.

"I'm very ready, Mrs. Smith," she said with a smile. She hit a few computer keys, and a gorgeous picture of fall in Wilmore, West Virginia, lit the screen. Replete with well-maintained wood frame houses and golden images of sun-washed leaves, the picture could have been a postcard. Most of the board members gasped with appreciation.

"My town is in West Virginia," she said, confidently glancing at each of the individuals around the table. She tapped the keyboard of her computer, and another picture of Wilmore appeared. "As you can see, we have a beautiful mountain as our backdrop." She touched her keypad again and a third image of the town appeared. This one was a shot taken around lunchtime when the streets were filled with people and the stores were open for business.

"Most of our commerce is still homegrown. Small shops owned by local people. My beauty salon is right there," she said, pointing at the doorway of her shop. Then, as if to downplay the significance of that, she quickly moved on to a slide of the next street down, which was the first street of neat, cookie-cutter houses, complete with flower beds in full bloom.

Tanner watched in growing amazement as Bailey went through slide after slide, telling the story of a wonderful, quiet, safe little town. The pictures were ordered in such a way as to masterfully lead the board members to recognize that the people who sustained and fostered this environment deserved to be rewarded with a small public park, designed to allow the entire town to participate in the rearing of its children. Expanding on the African proverb that it takes a village to raise a child, she gave illustrations of how adult members of the community had impacted her life. Then she showed how a park, a public meeting place, a source of recreation and a place for entertainment, could provide an even greater opportunity for the adults of Wilmore to participate in the growth and development of the children of their town.

Once she had the board enamored with her town and its people, she showed a blueprint-like sketch of a park, obviously created by software designed to make such things. The sketch included a pavilion, a stage and benches, all working with the plants and trees indigenous to their West Virginia county.

She then took a map of Wilmore, probably provided by Artie, and superimposed the park over the layout of the town, illustrating that a park in the center would be available to everyone.

Tanner observed her with fascination as she not only described a wholesome town and provided a reasonable facsimile of the kind of park that could best suit them, but she also proved herself to be a dependable, capable leader who would neither squander nor waste the foundation's money.

Pleased, he sat back on his chair, crossed his arms on his chest and watched her. With her hair pulled back in a tight chignon and just enough makeup to enhance her mysterious violet eyes, Bailey could stop traffic. Instead, she never took advantage of her beauty, frequently downplayed it and focused on using her education and intelligence. She was smart, educated and up for the challenges of a new business. He could see that from her comportment and the care and detail she put into this presentation. Smart enough to have gotten information from Amanda, she knew her audience, and she appealed to them, reeled them in. Now she nurtured them with facts as she made it very, very easy for them to decide to give her the money she needed.

Tanner smiled. She was a natural. Not just a natural-born leader, but an instinctive businessperson. He could almost feel the electricity created by the combination of her hard work and skilled presentation. She wasn't just good, she was great.

*Great.*

The simple word reverberated through him. This was what he had sensed about her all along, why she piqued his curiosity, why she drew him when he didn't want to be drawn. Bailey Stephenson wasn't an average woman. She wasn't an average anything. She was great and destined for greatness.

He realized then that she would probably have something bigger and better than his trucking company, and knew, watching her, that she would have an empire of sorts. In fact, with her looks and her hair, she could probably be her own spokesperson.

Just the thought of how far she would go, how high

she would climb, how good she could be, shot a thrill through him. It felt odd to be in on the ground floor of knowing somebody who would be great, before they actually became great. He was almost euphoric with the knowledge that he could see something that others might glimpse, but only a person who had traveled her journey would truly understand.

And he wanted to make love to her.

Which surprised him. He had always been very careful to keep work and play entirely separate. So he decided that since he wasn't really involved in her business, the strong desire he had to make love to her stemmed from a feeling of celebration, and appreciation for her. Those were not business emotions. They were personal, intimate desires, because in a sense he felt he knew her intimately simply from observing her. Observing her and understanding her, he realized he was aware of her in a way that no one else in her world probably could be, but he also recognized that because he understood her, she understood him. There was a reciprocation of some kind happening between them. And that's what excited him. The fact that he found someone he not only understood, but someone who also understood him.

When Bailey hazarded a glance in Tanner's direction, the look he gave her didn't merely fill her with confidence, it filled her with need. Sharp, sweet pangs of desire hit her. Not just because she wanted to make love to him, but because she sensed that he saw the image of herself she sometimes saw when she dared to really dream about everything she could be.

Recognizing what he saw, she felt vital and strong and sensual...which was irrelevant, she reminded herself, but somehow the notion wouldn't go away. The way he

looked at her was so sexual that she was having a hard
time concentrating on the grant application. The words
and phrases weren't coming naturally anymore. The feelings she had for Tanner superseded everything else.

She finished the presentation by handing out copies of
the grant application, which had been revised one final
time. She incorporated the blue prints and pictures she
had used that day, because she knew it wouldn't hurt for
the board to take away a visual image of her presentation
to think about while they pondered her park's fate.

But Mrs. Smith unexpectedly waved away her copy.
"I don't want that," she barked, and Bailey stopped dead
in her tracks. She saw Tanner coil, as if he would stand,
and she quickly shook her head, indicating that he
shouldn't do anything but should let her handle this.

"I thought you would appreciate copies of some of the
pictures I showed as well as the rough blueprint of the
proposed park to help you make your decision," she said
calmly, giving Mrs. Smith a look that was both friendly
and firm.

Mrs. Smith sighed heavily. "Honey, I've already made
my decision," she said, rising from her seat.

Bailey's heart stopped. Not only had the old woman
risen, but now she was walking to the door. Stunned by
both the rudeness of the departure and the fact that Mrs.
Smith hardly seemed to be giving them a chance, Bailey
stood mute.

"And the board doesn't really have to meet, either,"
she said, as she reached the door. Three men jumped up
to grab the handle for her. She waved them away, too.
"If I remember our charter, the final decision is mine,
anyway, so there's no sense in adding work to work."
She paused, caught Bailey's eye and said, "You get your
money. In fact, I can have Amanda go to accounting and

have them cut your check for the first installment of the money while you wait…that is, if you don't mind waiting.''

Nearly paralyzed with surprise, Bailey barely got out the words, ''No, we don't mind waiting.''

''Good, because your drawing was terrible. I want you to hire a landscape architect to actually design the park. I'll throw in an extra hundred thousand for that, and any left-over money can be used at your revitalization committee's discretion. Other installments will be made as your architect and contractors turn in requests for reimbursement. My legal staff will draw up contracts and have them mailed to you to put in your bid packages. Good day, Bailey,'' she said, this time actually opening the door, but before she walked through, she paused and faced Bailey again.

Her lips quirked as if it irked her to admit this, but ultimately she smiled and said, ''It was a pleasure to meet you.''

With that she walked out of the room and the members of her committee began to disburse. One by one, before they left the room, they approached Bailey with congratulations on her presentation and expressions of approval over her getting the grant money she wanted. The line thinned and eventually disappeared. At its end was Amanda.

A short red-haired woman with brown eyes and dressed in an emerald-green suit, Amanda was the picture of propriety. ''Congratulations,'' she said, shaking Bailey's hand. ''It's not often that Mrs. Smith changes her mind once she decides she dislikes someone. Your presentation must have been flawless.''

''Actually, it was more heartfelt than flawless,'' Bailey

confessed, then drew a long breath. "So what do we do now?"

"Just wait here. I'll go to accounting and set the wheels in motion for your check. It shouldn't be long, only about twenty minutes."

She left the room, and suddenly Bailey realized she and Tanner were alone. The silence echoed around her.

"You were magnificent," he said, his words resonating through the quiet room.

"Thanks," she said, busying herself with disassembling her computer, because she was acutely aware of him. She felt as if heat from him was arching to her, pulling her thoughts to him. "But I can't take all the credit. Wilmore speaks for itself."

"No, it doesn't," he said with a laugh. "Wilmore is a lovely town, but it needed someone to speak for it. You were a wonderful spokesperson. In fact," he said, rising from his seat to walk over to her, "watching you, I decided you should become the spokesperson for your salons, once you begin to spread out or to franchise."

She peered at him. "Really?"

"Sure," he said, cupping her upper arms and turning her to face him. "You know you're going to be great someday, don't you?"

She shook her head using that movement to take her mind off the heat spiraling through her just from the touch of his fingers on her arm. "Sometimes I get a clear picture of it. Other times, like when something I've done backfires or doesn't work out, I can't see it at all."

"That's all right. It's normal to have moments of doubt. The thing is you don't let those moments of doubt rule you, you remember moments like this to keep you going."

They were standing toe-to-toe, looking into each

other's eyes, and when he told her to remember moments like this to keep her going, Bailey knew that she would, but not for the reasons he expected. She wouldn't remember that a nameless board of directors saw a presentation, or even that a woman who disliked her unexpectedly approved of her. She would remember that someone she liked and respected recognized her talent. She would remember that he felt the need to tell her, to encourage her and maybe even to motivate her. She would remember that he was gloriously handsome, smelled like heaven and kissed better than anyone she'd ever known. Because he was only in her life for a few weeks, probably sent by fate to inspire her since he couldn't have a permanent relationship, Bailey had decided to remember everything, to keep it all close to her heart and to bring out the memories often. Because she knew there would never be another man like him in her life.

Some of what she was feeling must have shown in her expression, because he tilted his head in question. Then a smoky haze came into his eyes as if he finally deduced what she would remember from this day.

He said, "Sometimes the way you look at me is pure flattery, Bailey."

"Really?" she said, intending to be flippant and funny, but sounding breathless and hopeful.

"Yeah," he said, smiling like a man who could use a little flattery in his life. Though Bailey didn't have a clue why, she sensed it strongly enough that she knew she had to do something about it.

She stepped closer and straightened his tie with fingers that desperately needed to be busy. "I guess I'm going to have to work on my facial expressions, then. That was supposed to be my thank-you look."

"Thank-you look?" he asked.

She shrugged. "Yeah, you've helped me out a lot these past few weeks. I know it might have sometimes seemed I resented your interference, but I didn't. I appreciate everything you've done for us. Especially finding Mrs. Smith's foundation."

"Oh, shucks, ma'am, that was easy," he said, being silly, teasing her.

But Bailey sensed that, though he didn't want the praise or the thank-you, he needed to see that his efforts, no matter how simple to him, counted, *really counted.*

"No, it wasn't. You have to have made some faithful friends to have been able to get us that appointment with Mrs. Smith."

He laughed. "Bailey, you did all the work here."

She shook her head. "It wouldn't have mattered if you hadn't found us a way to get to Mrs. Smith."

"I have some good friends. It's one of the perks of being rich and formerly famous."

"No it isn't," she protested. "Only people who can be good friends have good friends. Don't downplay what you do. It takes very special people to establish and keep relationships like that," she said, stepping closer. "And I happen to think you're wonderful."

He knew by looking into her eyes that she did. Those bright violet-blue orbs of hers couldn't keep a secret. The knowledge that she had such extraordinary feelings for him trickled through him like water trying to create a stream in a desert. When he remembered his first thoughts about her, that if she liked him it wouldn't be superficially, the trickle turned into a steam and the stream soon became a rush.

He laid his hand on her cheek. "Thanks."

She smiled. "You're welcome."

Feelings that Tanner thought long dead began to rise

up inside him. He realized that the reason he believed he could have a permanent relationship with this woman was that she was honest and genuine. If they had a problem, she would tell him. She wouldn't let it fester until there was no way to repair their relationship. She wouldn't hurl accusations at him when it was too late to fix them. If he decided to give his heart to her, she wouldn't hand it back a few years later.

"Bailey, Tanner?" Amanda called from the conference room door.

They broke apart like guilty teenagers, both pivoting to face the door.

"Yes?" Bailey asked breathlessly.

"Here's your check," Amanda said, walking into the room. "Congratulations again."

"Thanks," Bailey said, and Tanner suspected she had to resist the urge to hug the check to her bosom. "One hundred thousand dollars," she said. "I almost can't believe it."

"Well, it sounds like it's going for a very good cause," Amanda said, then turned toward the door. "I'll escort you out."

"Great," Bailey replied. She folded the check and stuffed it into her purse, and Tanner watched her, feeling like a man in a trance. Part of him cautiously, hopefully, tiptoed toward the belief that maybe he didn't have to leave her behind. But the sensible part knew that couldn't be true. Now that she had her grant, her work in Wilmore was only beginning. She couldn't go anywhere and he was leaving for Florida as soon as he could get himself packed.

"You know, you've got to hire a landscape architect," he softly reminded her.

"Yeah," she said, but she grinned. "And I have just the guy."

"The guy?" he asked as Bailey began to follow Amanda and he followed Bailey.

"A friend from college. His name is Dennis."

Tanner stopped. "Dennis?"

"Yeah, Dennis," she flippantly replied without seeming to notice that Tanner had stopped walking and stood paralyzed as if frozen to the floor.

How could he leave her when she was about to make the biggest mistake of her life?

# Chapter Nine

Bailey and Tanner sat in silence as she drove the SUV out of Charlottesville. Maneuvering through traffic took her full concentration, and she didn't notice how somber Tanner was until they were miles from the city, riding down a country road on their way to Wilmore again. They could have taken a more direct route on highways built for speed, but she suddenly wasn't in any hurry to get home. She knew that once they were home he could leave. There was no reason for him to stay in Wilmore anymore. Not only had his car been repaired and the erosion and sedimentation controls on his parents' property been built, but now his duties to the revitalization committee had been fulfilled.

He could leave, and she hoped the reason he was thoughtful, almost brooding was that he wasn't sure he wanted to go.

"Turn here!" he said suddenly.

Bailey peered at him. "Here, where?"

"Up there," he said, pointing at a winding road that sat beside a sign announcing Windmere Country Club.

"You want to go to a country club?"

He drew in a long breath. "No. But I have some things I want to think about, and I think best when I'm outside."

"At a country club?" she asked dubiously, but she did turn onto the road and begin the journey along the tree-lined entryway.

"Playing golf," he clarified.

For some reason or another that made her laugh. "And what am I supposed to do while you play golf?"

"You're going to play, too," he said, then jumped out of her SUV when she brought it to a stop in the club's parking lot.

Bailey followed him, trying to catch him as he strode into the main building, which was actually a Cape Cod house. Painted pale yellow and sporting forest-green shutters, it resembled a home more than a place of business.

"Tanner, take a look at me," she said, scampering to keep up with him as he strode along. "Not only am I wearing a suit, but I have on heels...and panty hose!" she said, her eyes widening as she realized all that could mean.

He stopped and gave her the slow, sexy smile that nearly buckled her knees. "So take them off."

"And golf naked," she said, not about to fall victim to that smile until she understood what was going on here.

"Now, there's a thought," he said, then continued to stride up to the entrance. He held the door for her. "But places like this are usually populated by old men looking for an afternoon in the sun. I wouldn't want to have to be doing CPR every ten minutes. Instead I'll just buy you shorts and a T-shirt in the pro shop.''

As always he made it sound easy and normal, and for him it seemed to be. A one-hundred-dollar bill got him the privilege of paying another two hundred dollars for them to play golf on this exclusive club course. He paid seventy-five dollars apiece for khaki shorts for each of them and fifty dollars for a golf shirt she knew with absolute certainty she would never wear again.

"This is ridiculous," Bailey muttered, her arms loaded down with shorts, shirts and two pair of golf shoes while Tanner rummaged through the visors.

"Wait until you see what I'm about to pay for visors. Here, get a load of this," he said, displaying the price tag for a white terry cloth visor decorated with pink golf tees.

She gasped. "That's criminal."

"No, it's good business. Look around you, Bailey," he said, then glanced around himself as if to show her the way. "This place caters to people who have money. If you don't want to pay fifty dollars for an ugly shirt, you shouldn't be here."

"I shouldn't be here," she mumbled as they walked to the cash register.

Without waiting for a total or even for the old gentleman clerk to ring up their purchases, Tanner handed his credit card across the counter.

"I'm going to pay for mine," Bailey said, dropping her things in front of the small, discreet cash register and reaching for her purse.

"No way," Tanner said, grabbing her hand before she could open the snap. "This is my idea. I pay."

"You're just saying that because you know I'm broke."

He laughed. "I'm about to golf with a woman who will someday be on *Pinnacle* explaining to a CNN interviewer how she got her start in life. I figure these golf clothes—" he glanced around again "—and this outing ought to win me at least honorable mention somewhere in the show."

"You're bribing me?"

"Trying to stay in your good graces."

With that he walked out of the pro shop into the lobby again and asked the gentleman clerk about a locker room. Another hundred dollars not only got them access to the men's and women's changing area, it also got them keys to unrented lockers for the afternoon. Bailey climbed out of her suit, panty hose and pumps and into the khaki shorts, ugly green-purple-and-beige T-shirt and white terry cloth visor. Then she looked at herself in the full-length mirror and burst out laughing.

"You look great," Tanner said, as she walked out into the afternoon sunshine from the backdoor of the locker area.

"Yeah, you, too," Bailey teased because his shirt was every bit as ugly as hers, but the truth was he did look handsome. Even tacky clothes couldn't hide or diminish his sun-bleached hair, brilliant green eyes, and perfect physique, and he looked like a young successful man on a golf outing. He was a million times more attractive than any of the guys in plaid sans-a-belt slacks, and, at least for the afternoon, he was hers.

Which, she supposed, was the real bottom line to being out here right now. He said he had some things to think about, but before she got her hopes up that he might be considering staying, she knew she had to face the fact that this side trip might have a much simpler purpose. He could be doing nothing more on this golf course than delaying the inevitable: when they got home, he would leave for Florida. They would probably never see each other again. That made him as sad as it made her, and he wasn't quite ready to face that yet. So here they were on a golf course, taking advantage of every minute they had left together.

That reasoning probably explained why he had been so somber on the drive over. He wasn't thinking about changing his mind, he was thinking about preserving something for the future. If she were smart, she would do exactly what Tanner appeared to be doing: make a good memory from this afternoon. No stress. No demands. Just fun.

"I mean it," Tanner insisted as a caddie brought out the clubs Tanner had also rented. "You really look cute."

"Yeah, right."

Following Tanner's example, Bailey took a set of clubs from a young attendant, hooked them over her shoulder and began walking in the direction of the bay of golf carts. When they reached the closest one, she slid her golf bag into the rear holder, then jumped into the passenger side.

"How do you even know I play golf?" she asked, when Tanner jerked the little white car to a start and began driving to the first tee.

"You played in college," he said simply, but something about the way he said it made her feel awkward.

"What else do you know about me that I don't know you know?" Bailey asked, hopping out of the vehicle when they reached their destination.

"Not much," Tanner said. He punched his tee into the soft ground and set a ball on top of it. Then he chose a driver, tried it out by swinging at air and positioned himself in front of his ball. With one strong, swishing slice, he took his shot. The ball sailed across the perfect blue sky and landed immediately in front of the green.

"Damn," he muttered, yanking his tee from the dirt.

"What's 'damn' about that?" Bailey asked incredulously, staring at the place his ball landed as she further shielded her eyes from the sun by hooking her hand at the brim of her visor. "It looks like you're about a foot off the green."

"Yeah, well, in case you didn't notice, for me to get that close, this must be a deceptively short fairway. If I was on my A game I would have hit that green."

"Well, excuse me, Tiger Woods, but if you play that well, you are in for a long afternoon. I think anything under a six on a hole is spectacular. I don't start griping about shots until I get into double digits."

She took one practice swing, and, satisfied, she stepped up to the ball. She positioned herself and took her shot, then watched as her ball bounced pitifully across the fairway like a stone skipped across a lake.

He gave her a long-suffering stare. "I thought you said you played in college."

She smiled. "I never said I played in college," she said, returning the rented driver to its slot in the bag. "Somebody else *told* you I played in college."

Tanner boarded the golf cart. "And that bothers you?"

"A little."

"I would think you would be flattered that I liked you enough to go in search of information," he said, then revved the cart's engine and set them off in the direction of her ball.

"Is that what happened?" she asked, reminding herself to keep this light and friendly because she not only didn't want to get into an argument, she didn't want to get her hopes up.

He jerked the cart to a stop on the path across from her ball. "Something like that."

"And here I thought you might have just been nosy."

He grinned shamelessly. "Well, that's part of it."

"And did you get all the information you needed?"

"Nobody could explain you completely, Bailey," Tanner said with a chuckle. "Go hit your ball."

Bailey jumped out of the cart, chose a club from her bag then trudged from the cart path to her ball, which was dead center in the fairway.

"Hey, at least I'm in bounds," she called to Tanner who only shook his head in wonder. She swung the club. It caught the ball on the underside and lifted it skyward. For a few seconds it sailed nicely, then it began an arc of descent and plopped down a few feet to the right of Tanner's ball.

"I guess I can't complain about that," Tanner said as she slid onto the passenger seat. "Nice shot."

"Everybody gets a miracle every once in a while," she said, but she was proud of herself. She hadn't been the best golfer on her college team, but she had been a stable, steady player, and she remembered liking that feeling. "You know, if you would give me a few pointers and coach me a little on the next few shots, maybe some of this would come back to me."

He peeked at her. "You think so?"

"Sure," she said. "What could it hurt?"

*My sanity,* Tanner thought. It could definitely hurt my sanity. He had brought her out here so that he could think through what, if anything, he should do about her hiring her ex-lover, the man who had broken her heart, to be the landscape architect on her pet project. Instead he found he couldn't think at all because she looked ridiculously adorable in her ugly shirt, and she was funny. Witty. Fun to be around in a common ordinary sort of way. The kind of way that a man wants to have fun with the woman he will be with permanently. Now she wanted him to study and critique the positions of her arms and long, beautiful legs. Not to mention the swing of her hips. But first he would have to stand behind her to check her grip on the club. The only way to do that was to press himself against her back and put his arms around her.

Yeah, this was going to be peachy. He had brought them out here to get time to figure out how to keep her from making a big mistake, and instead he was only finding more ways and reasons to be close to her. Not just emotionally and mentally now but also physically.

Like he said, peachy.

He chipped his ball onto the green, watched it glide gracefully toward the pin and stop less than a foot away.

"You're going to get a birdie," Bailey said joyfully.

"After that chip, I'd better," Tanner said, walking to the cart where he deposited his iron and retrieving his putter. He expected to find Bailey at least lining herself up for her shot when he turned to face her. Instead, she stood smiling at him.

"What?"

"Gimme some help," she said, coaxing him. "Come on, I want to get a chip like yours. I want to par the hole."

He drew in a long breath, not wanting to explain he couldn't snuggle up to her after the feelings he had been having about her all day. It was going to be hard enough to leave her when the time came. He didn't want to be making any more clear and graphic memories, in addition to the ones he already had.

"Just take the shot, Bailey. I'm sure you'll be fine."

"But what if I'm not," she said, almost whining. "Come on. I want to par the hole."

He could see she didn't understand the ramifications of his reminding her of some of the basics, then wondered if he hadn't imagined all those wonderful things he saw in her eyes back in Mrs. Smith's conference room. If she had the kind of physical and emotional feelings for him he was sure he saw shining in her eyes, then she had to know snuggling up would be a disaster and she wouldn't suggest it. Of course, it wouldn't be the first time he had misunderstood or misinterpreted a woman's reaction to him. And if he continued to refuse her and she dragged the reason out of him, he could embarrass himself mightily. Better to just give her the damned lesson.

"All right," he said, sighing as he trudged away from the cart. He stood behind her, noted the angle of her ball to the hole, then put his hands on her hips and shifted her slightly so that she was aiming better. "Stand a bit to the left."

"Like this?" she said, wiggling her hips as she repositioned herself.

He gritted his teeth. "Exactly."

"Okay," she said. "Now what?"

He sighed inwardly, then bit the bullet and stood immediately behind her so that he could take her hands and appropriately place them on her club. Feeling his chest pressed against her back and the way her shoulders molded into him, he looked down at the grip they had created together, and he got the oddest sensation of rightness. Their hands together, entwined, looked perfect. So damned right.

"Your hold on the club is good," he said, grateful that he could step back away from her. "Now, just bring the club back slowly, and keep your head down so that that club face goes under the ball and doesn't scrape the top."

"Okay," Bailey said, then wiggled her hips as if getting comfortable with her stance, but for Tanner the movement affected him as drastically as if she were snuggling against him. "I remember most of that. I can do it."

"You bet you can," Tanner said, squeezing his eyes shut, praying that she made an excellent shot because he certainly didn't want to cuddle up to her again.

She drew the club back and he held his breath. Then she brought it down and smacked the underside of the ball. The little white orb lifted gracefully and plopped down in the center of the green.

"Yes!" she said, doing a victory dance. "I'm on the green in three and I'm going to par this hole."

"If you make your putt," Tanner observed, not really thinking about what he was saying.

"Of course I'm going to make my putt," she said, striding to the cart to return her iron and grab her putter. "You're going to help me."

"Bailey, you're doing fine," Tanner said, holding back a groan of desperation.

"My second shot was a gift from God. That chip I just made I did well because you helped me." She glanced over at him. "I really want to par this hole," she said, holding his gaze, looking so sweet and sincere that his heart lurched. "Please."

He sighed. "All right," he agreed, walking with her onto the green. Because she was farther from the hole than he was, her shot was first. Tanner walked behind the flag and gauged the lay of her ball in relation to the cup. He stooped down and studied the contour of the green and the height of the grass, calculating not only the trajectory, but also how fast the ball would travel, given the height and thickness of the grass.

"Okay," he said, rising and joining her at her ball. "Here's the deal. The ball's probably going to go right because of a slight grade you can't see from up here."

"I should have studied the green," she said pensively.

"That's all right, I did it. Let's just get this over with," he said, then stood behind her. "Because the ball's going to angle to the right, you need to shift a little bit like this and aim for that little brown spot. That's about where it will curve and start downward to the cup."

"Okay," she said, nodding, comfortably leaning into him so he could position her.

He closed his eyes. But instead of feeling awkward and wishing to get this over with, he let himself savor the moment. To him, this was what a real relationship would be about. Being a part of the common, ordinary, inconsequential things of each other's lives. Like a golf stroke. He let himself inhale the scent of her hair. He let himself soak in the feeling of her shoulders pressed into him. He let his hands slide down her arms on their way to helping her grip the club.

"There," he said, but his voice came out hoarse and whispered.

"Thanks," she said, slightly breathless.

Tanner realized she was only now recognizing what was really happening between them, and he took two paces back, away from her.

"Okay, slowly drag the club back about twelve inches

then just tap the ball, because the green's going to provide the momentum.''

Bailey did as he instructed, bringing the club back and
tapping her ball. It started off slowly, but, as Tanner pre-
dicted, when it hit the little brown spot it curved to the
right and picked up speed, quickly traveling down the
slope and dropping into the hole.

"Yeeeeessss!" Bailey said, jumping for joy. "I did it.
The first time I played golf in three years and I parred
the first hole!"

"Yes, you did," Tanner said, walking over to his own
ball. He gauged his position, figured in the green speed
and tapped his ball. It also dropped into the cup.

"And you got a birdie!" Bailey said, clapping as if
they had won an award.

Her enthusiasm went through him like a knife. He
wanted this. He wanted a life with someone who could
enjoy a meaningless game. He wanted a life with someone who could be happy and jump for joy. Yet, not only
did he have to walk away from her, but he was going to
have to sit by and watch her bring her ex-boyfriend back
to be the landscaper for her park because he didn't have
a clue how to talk her out of it. Tanner himself had almost set it up for this guy, a guy who had hurt her, to
reap some pretty nice benefits. She wouldn't even be getting this project off the ground if Tanner hadn't found
the funding.

"I'm thrilled," he said, realizing every ounce of his
frustration had come out in that one simple sentence,
though he hadn't wanted it to.

"You should be," Bailey said curiously. "But I can
see that you're not."

"I'm fine," Tanner said, wishing now that he could

be away from her, because all he was doing was tormenting himself. "Let's just get going to the next tee."

Bailey stood frozen. "Hey, wait a minute," she said, struggling to catch up with him. "Don't make this sound like torture. You're the one who wanted to play golf. Not me. You're the one who went to the extreme of buying these ugly shirts. Not me. So don't go getting all grouchy and uptight. For Pete's sake you just got a birdie. You should be dancing for joy."

He knew she was right. But he also knew she didn't understand half of what was going on inside him right now, because he didn't understand it, either.

"A birdie and you're grouchy," she muttered, sliding into the cart, which Tanner immediately brought to life.

"I'm not grouchy," he said, endeavoring to sound sane and normal rather than like the idiot he probably looked to her. "I'm just a little pensive this afternoon. A little thoughtful. I told you I needed to come out here to think. You're the one who turned it into a game."

"So what?" she said, then turned her face into the breeze created by their moving cart. "It is a game."

He wished. He really wished.

"I can't believe you said that," he mumbled, then pressed his foot a little harder on the accelerator to get them to the next tee. "You're going to have to start taking things a little more seriously if you plan on achieving your goals."

She gaped at him. "Tanner, how can you say that! I do take things seriously!" She peered at him curiously. "And you know I take things seriously!"

"Oh, yeah?" he said, then jumped out of the cart. "That's why you're bringing an old boyfriend back to be your landscape architect."

Bailey's mouth fell open in surprise. Equally surprised

that he had come right out and said that, Tanner didn't hang around for her response. He jumped out of the cart, grabbed his driver, punched his tee into the dirt—ball and all—and slammed off his shot. His club cracked the ball and sent it skyward. Because this fairway was longer and also had a dog leg, Tanner didn't even really see where it fell.

"I'm bringing Dennis in to be my architect because he is very, very good."

"Oh, forget about the fact that he hurt you."

She gaped at him. "Tanner, it is infuriating that you know so much about me."

"Like you don't know everything there is to know about me?"

"No one knows everything there is to know about you," Bailey incredulously replied. "You've as much as admitted that to me a hundred times. You skirt right on the edge of actually explaining why you and Emmalee got divorced but never tell me. You talk about your business, by explaining to me what you think I should do, but never really say anything concrete like how many trucks you had, where your corporate office was, how many employees you had...who bought the damned thing. It's like you think your life is supposed to be this stellar mystery that no one has the right to know."

"All right," he said, shoving his driver back into his golf bag. "You want to know what happened with me and Emmalee, I'll tell you. I hurt my leg, I lost my job and I went a little nuts needing to prove to myself that just because I blew out my knee and spent a year getting surgeries it didn't mean I couldn't still be Superman. I put so much time into looking for the best place to put the compensation I got from my contract that I ignored my wife. By the time she asked me to leave she despised me. Because while I was making myself feel better I made her feel worthless.''

He stopped, drew a long breath. It hurt so much to admit it, he actually felt tears spring to his eyes. He drew a long breath, shoving all the feelings down again, the way he always did, because the regrets were pointless.

"There. Are you happy now?''

"Oh, Tanner,'' Bailey said, sympathetic when he didn't want her to be. "Your whole world had crumbled. You had a right to be a little off your game.''

"No one has a right to make another person feel worthless. Especially not the person you're supposed to love.''

"Did you ever stop to think that she's the one who dropped the ball? Did you ever stop to think that she should have been supporting you?''

He swallowed. "No. I was the great one, Bailey. Of the two of us I was the one with the confidence and drive. Emma depended on me, and I let her down.''

Bailey shook her head. "It takes two to tango, Tanner.''

"And that's why you find it so easy to forgive this Dennis character? Because you take the blame for the fact that he stole money from you?''

Bailey shook her head. "In his mind, he didn't steal from me. I thought I was lending him a year's tuition. He thought I was giving it to him.''

"Oh, that's a hot one,'' Tanner said, so furious he could spit and not even sure why.

"It's not a hot one. It's the truth. Because we were living together, and had a stake in each other's lives, he genuinely believed I was giving him the money.''

"And when you broke up and you no longer had that stake in each other's lives, that had no impact on him.''

"It also had no impact on a judge," Bailey admitted honestly. "We had no papers, Tanner. No written agreement. I couldn't prove it was a loan, and things I had said, things I had to testify to in court did give Dennis the impression that I saw the money as community property."

Tanner only stared at her. "You are so naive. He ripped you off. Now you're giving him a chance to do it again."

"No, I'm giving him a job," Bailey said coolly, obviously getting angry, too, but Tanner didn't care. He was jealous and frustrated, and lashing out at her seemed to be the only thing he could do.

"You're giving him a place in your life."

"And that bothers you?"

He drew a long breath. "It bothers me because I think, as a businessperson, you are making a big mistake. You're going to make enough mistakes, Bailey, without trusting someone who doesn't deserve to be trusted."

"Is that your professional opinion?"

He sighed, glad to have the professional excuse to keep him in her business when he had no right to be. "Yes."

"Well, I think you're wrong, and I think from here on out you should stay out of my life." With that she shoved her club back into the golf bag. "Let's go home."

He shook his head. "No, you take the cart back and you go home," he said softly, quietly.

"And how will you get back?"

He looked at her. "I always find my way, Bailey. I don't need you."

Her chin lifted and she held his gaze. "Actually, Tanner, that's the real problem. You don't *need* anybody."

# Chapter Ten

"What are you doing?"

Tanner glanced up from packing and saw his mother standing in his bedroom door. "What does it look like I'm doing?"

"Well, you have suitcases out and all your shirts are lying on the bed. Either you're taking inventory or you're planning a trip somewhere."

Tanner only looked at his mother. "You've got to get out more."

"Don't I know it. So where are you going?"

"Florida."

"Oh," she said, strolling into the room. "How long are you staying?"

"Forever," he said, then peeked over to see his mother fingering the collar of one of his shirts. He didn't even have to see the look in her eyes to know what she was feeling or to get the rush of guilt.

"Come on. We made this deal months ago. I'll get a big house close to the Gulf of Mexico. You and Dad will visit me instead of me visiting you. You can stay all winter if you like.''

"Winters in Wilmore are too beautiful to leave."

"Winters in Wilmore are cold and wet. You need to go."

"No," she said, shaking her head. "It seems like you're the one who needs to go." She glanced over at Tanner. "Care to tell me why?"

"You know why."

"No. Not really. Aside from that whole warmer climate excuse, I never did figure out why you have to go."

Tanner drew a long breath. "Mom, I'm not going to get into this."

"Okay, then satisfy my curiosity about why you suddenly have to leave when this morning you weren't even talking about it yet."

"This morning I wasn't sure how everything would go with the grant from Smith Foundation. Now, I know. Bailey got her money. I can leave."

"Oh," Doris McConnell said, taking a seat on the bed beside Tanner's suitcase. "Bailey got her grant. So you can leave."

"Exactly."

"Nice girl that Bailey."

"Yes, she is."

"Sweet, homespun…and yet talented. She's a wonderful businessperson."

"You don't know the half of it." He shook his head. "The woman is a phenomenon. She wants to start some kind of beauty salon franchise, and I think she can do it. She's brilliant. She thinks on her feet. She falls down but forces herself back up again. Someday we're all going to be saying, I knew her when."

Puzzled, Tanner's mother only stared at him. "So why don't you want to stay and help her?"

Tanner laughed. "Because I like her."

Doris shook her head fiercely. "No, that should mean you want to stay. If you like her you should want to help her, because she likes you, too. I can see it."

"That's just the point. She does like me, too. But if she would get involved with me, I would try to take over. I'd boss her around, give advice she doesn't want. I would make a mess of things."

The way he'd done that afternoon. After hours of watching her make a presentation that proved she was going to be great someday, he didn't trust her enough to let her choose her own workforce. He'd interfered, he'd started a fight, and he'd proven what Emma had said all along. He was a control freak. Bailey's parting shot was way, way off the mark. The problem wasn't that Tanner didn't need anybody. The problem was that he needed people so much he was afraid to let them make their own decisions. Because he was jealous of an old boyfriend, fearful of Bailey bringing Dennis back into her life, he didn't respect Bailey's right to run her project the best way she knew how. He had been dead wrong to tell her what to do, yet he couldn't seem to stop himself.

"Tanner, you just sold a multimillion-dollar business. Has it ever once occurred to you that some of your input might be good for her? You know business law and accounting, and even how to deal with the IRS. There are a million ways you could help her. In fact, if you helped her she would have time to have a relationship. Because we both know that without help somewhere, she's not going to have much of a life during start-up."

Tanner had never even stopped to consider that Bailey wouldn't have time for him. All his thoughts had been so focused on avoiding the relationship that he almost forgot how busy she would be.

"It wouldn't be right for me to interfere," he said, clinging to the part of the problem he always acknowledged, because his mother's observation confused him. But more than that he knew his reasoning was correct. He was bossy and jealous, and he didn't know how to stop himself from trying to get everybody to do everything the way he thought it should be done.

"Besides," he said, changing the subject. "I'm retiring. I worked for this. I earned it. I want to go to Florida, have a boat, take groups out to sea. It's all I've talked about for the past ten years. I can't just give up my dream."

"Well, if you're so worried about interfering and so hell-bent on retiring. Why don't you look at this another way?"

"And what way is that?"

"If you're so sure Bailey's destined for success, you're perfect for her because you could be a stay-at-home dad."

Again the observation resonated through Tanner, throwing him off balance. He had never considered that he could be a stay-at-home dad. He had never even considered that with Bailey he could be a dad. Not only did the thought fill him with awe, but in a weird sort of way it also made perfect sense. He rose from the bed and began to pace.

"You have a problem with being a stay-at-home dad?" Doris asked suspiciously.

"No," he said, and realized it was true. The oddest tingle of recognition rippled through him because his mother's simple suggestion might actually solve his problem. He could keep himself from interfering in Bailey's business by becoming her *personal* support system. He wouldn't have to rule or ruin her life. He could love her. He could simply be there for her. And if he were busy with a baby or two, he wouldn't have to worry about meddling, particularly not if he had a part-time charter business filling the need to do something professional.

Strange, wonderful relief poured through him. He didn't have to be alone anymore. Everything he wanted really was his for the taking.

"So..." Tanner's mother said encouragingly.

"So I think I love you," Tanner said to his mother, bent down and placed a smacking kiss on her cheek.

"Don't tell me. Go tell Bailey."

"Okay." Tanner said, turning toward his bedroom door. He was nearly thunderstruck with his discoveries, bubbling with joy and anticipation, but another thought occurred to him before he got to the door. He faced his mother again. "Mom, even if Bailey agrees to marry me, this doesn't mean I'm not going to Florida eventually."

"It doesn't?"

"I still want the boat, it was the carrot that got me through ten years in trucking, and I'm not giving it up. I think it will be easier for me if I have something to keep me busy so I won't try to tinker in what Bailey's doing. But more than that, I think Bailey would have a much easier time establishing herself in a bigger city, with a different kind of clientele than she has here. I think," he said, wondering why he was only realizing now that what was good for him was also good for her, "that moving away will be good for her career."

His mother's face collapsed into a horrified expression. "But Bailey belongs in Wilmore."

"Wilmore takes advantage of Bailey," Tanner said, recognizing it was true and that he had known it all along.

"She needs me," he said, suddenly deeply understanding it was true, and feeling strong, proud and in control of himself and his life. "And I need her. But it's an equal partnership. Neither one of us would ever take advantage of the other. That's why we both need to be out of this little town. Not only because it's stifling her but also because...well, because I've always needed to be gone."

When he drove by Bailey's salon on his way to her apartment, he noticed that a light was on in the back of the shop. Thinking she might be catching up on paperwork, he drove around to the rear lot, and sure enough her SUV was parked by the back entry. But when he jogged up the steps and tried the door it was locked.

Because there was a bell at the front entry, and not wanting to scare her since it was after ten o'clock at night, Tanner walked around to the front. Before ringing the bell, though, he tried the door and it opened.

He was just about to call out a greeting when he heard her feminine giggle coming from a back room. Before he could stop it, jealousy flared up in him. He always thought that giggle was reserved for him. Thinking that another man made her laugh that way sent a shaft of pure unadulterated possessiveness through him.

"Oh, June, you look wonderful."

"Thanks, Bailey," June Harmon said, and Tanner stopped dead in his tracks as relief ricocheted through him because she wasn't with a man. But a feeling of foolishness followed quickly on its heels. He knew better than to think Bailey would spend the day with him, look at him with love in her eyes and then jump right into the arms of another man as if nothing had happened.

He drew a long breath. He had to get over this jealousy and fear that she really didn't love him.

"Bailey, I don't know how I'm going to pay you for this," June began, but Bailey quickly interrupted her.

"You're not going to pay me!" she adamantly insisted. "I needed the experience of gathering the hair and finding a good vendor to make the wigs for me. You're helping me."

"I don't know what to say," June replied, and because her voice was a tight whisper Tanner barely heard her.

"You don't have to say anything."

"Bailey, you don't understand. Everybody in the entire world thought I should be grateful to be alive when the chemotherapy worked. And I was," June quickly assured Bailey. "And I wasn't upset about losing my hair because of my looks."

"June, you don't have to tell me this stuff—"

"Yes, I do," June quickly replied. "You're the only person who understood that without my hair, every time I went outside my door I reminded people that I was sick. I don't mind that everybody knows I was sick. I just want people to stop pitying me and scaring my kids. I don't want to be the object of everybody's pity until my hair grows back and everybody forgets."

"Well, now you don't have to be," Bailey said brightly, but Tanner heard the forced tone of her voice and knew she was struggling to hold back her emotions. He stood frozen, not sure what to do, only knowing that he had intruded on something very, very private, and that if he made his presence known now he would embarrass June more than Bailey.

Quietly, carefully, he returned to the front door. He opened it, rang the bell to announce himself, then called, "Hey, anybody here?"

A few seconds of silence passed before Bailey said, "We're back here."

As if he hadn't been there, hadn't heard any of the conversation, he strode to the rear of the shop and pulled open the curtain.

"Bailey," he greeted with a nod. "June," he added, smiling at her. "Hey, nice hair. Bailey just cut that for you?"

June self-consciously fingered her new wig, but Bailey said, "Yes, actually, I did just cut it for her. We were looking for a new hairstyle for June that went with the shape of her face."

"You did a great job," Tanner said.

"Thanks," June replied. "And thank you, Bailey," she said, rising from the old salon chair. The thing was so ragged and torn, Tanner was sure it was sitting by the back door for disposal and Bailey had taken advantage of it to keep June's secret.

"But I have to get going or the kids will get worried."

"You have a ride home?" Tanner asked.

June shrugged. "I'm walking. It's not far."

"I know," Tanner began, but Bailey stopped him with a quick shake of her head. Understanding that Bailey was trying to tell him that June was working desperately to save her pride, Tanner smiled and said, "Have a nice walk."

"Thanks. And thanks again, Bailey," she said before she slipped out the back door.

When she was gone, the small storage room grew quiet. Bailey grabbed a broom and started sweeping up the hair she had probably trimmed from the wig. Tanner stood frozen. Every time he thought he knew everything there was to know about Bailey Stephenson, she surprised him.

"That was really nice of you."

Bailey shrugged. "A lot of times I'll open the shop at night to help out a busy mother."

"No, Bailey, I got here a couple of minutes ago. I heard."

"Well, don't go spreading it around," Bailey said as if exasperated. "June's had a really hard time. When I realized that part of the problem was she hated the fact that her hats were a constant reminder to everyone that she was sick, I figured getting the wig made was the least I could do."

"It was very nice of you."

"It wasn't anything anybody else who had the resources wouldn't have done. I have some unusual talents and some unusual opportunities, I like to use them."

Not quite sure what to do or even what to say now, Tanner stood staring at her while she bent to scoop up the swept hair.

"So, why are you here?" she asked.

He shrugged. "I came here for two reasons. First, to apologize."

She peeked at him. "So apologize."

He drew a long breath. "I'm sorry."

"That's all right. I'm starting to realize it's your nature to be a pain in the butt."

"Well, all that's going to stop," Tanner said, but as the words were coming out of his mouth, he glanced around the old back room, remembered what she had done for June, and what his mother had said about Bailey belonging in Wilmore. Strange feelings began to vibrate through him, and he wondered if she really could do better in a bigger city with a different kind of clientele. He was reminded of the story of the man who helped a butterfly escape its cocoon before it was time. He thought he was doing a good deed, but all he did was interrupt

the natural flow of things. And when he did, the butterfly
died.

"I actually talked about it with my mother tonight."

That made her laugh. "Why?"

"Because she thinks I should help you."

"And you don't?"

"Well, though it sounded good in theory, right now I
don't know."

"Why don't you let me be the judge of that? How do
you plan to help me?"

He couldn't tell her that. Even though the plan seemed
solid and right at his mother's house, and even though
he knew that if they didn't make this alliance right now
he would lose her, he also knew he couldn't tell her. He
couldn't taunt her with marriage and babies and Sunday
afternoons on the boat, things they couldn't have, because
it would be cruel. The plan that seemed so good at his
mother's house wouldn't work. He couldn't take her
away. That would be the worst form of interference of
all.

"My first thought was that I would pay off your business loan."

She looked at him. "The shop wouldn't be mine?"

"It isn't yours now. It belongs to you and the bank."

He could almost feel his joy floating out of him because this wasn't going to work. By asking her to move
away with him he was reordering her life, doing what
Emma said he always did, and that knowledge went
through him like a knife. He was sucking Bailey into his
life and dropping her life as if it were of little conse-
quence. Exactly what Emmalee had told him he did.

He drew a long breath. Took a pace back. "Look,
you're right—all of this is a bad idea." He tried to smile
but failed miserably, swallowed and took another step

back. "I'm sorry, Bailey. I'm sorry that I led you on, I'm sorry that I keep telling you what to do. You're right. It is my nature. I see the way I think things should be and I take over." He tried to smile again. "For better or for worse," he said and wondered why the hell he'd chosen that particular phaseology, "it's just the way I am. I'm sorry I can't change." He took another step back. "Really, really, really sorry."

"Tanner, wait!" Bailey cried because with the last "sorry," he slipped through the curtain and began to stride to her front door. "Wait!" she cried again, running after him.

When he stopped by the salon door, she said, "I get the feeling that you're talking about more here than my salon."

Looking like a man desperate to get away, he ran his hand along the back of his neck. "It was a stupid idea."

"I don't know that. I mean, we haven't discussed it. There might be points of compromise." She knew there was a devastating pleading in her voice. She couldn't stop it. Something, some damned thing had happened to make it impossible for him to commit to another woman after Emmalee. She sensed this every time they were on the verge of breaking through, because every time his pulling back became more clear, more obvious.

Knowing she had no choice, Bailey said, "Tanner, I love you. I think I started falling in love with you the minute I met you."

He turned to face her, his expression hopeful so Bailey continued.

"Right at this moment I would give up absolutely everything for you."

Tanner squeezed his eyes shut and groaned. "Don't say that, Bailey."

She ran to him and caught his arm to keep him from turning away. "It's true. I honest to God love you. I will do anything for you. Just tell me what it is I need to do and I will do it."

"What you need to do is find somebody that you can love who won't ask you to make huge compromises or change your life." He paused, caught her gaze. "I'm not that man, Bailey," he said, holding her gaze, his hands wrapped around her forearms. Then, as if he couldn't help himself, he used his grip on her arms to lever her forward and upward and press his mouth on hers. In a long, desperate kiss, he communicated an almost hopeless love to her, then he dropped her arms and spun around. He grabbed the doorknob, jerked open the door and ran out into the night.

Bailey bolted after him. "Tanner, no! Wait!" she cried, but he didn't stop walking. Long, determined strides took him away from her. Bailey froze to the spot. He really was going and she couldn't stop him. She didn't want to stop him because he was right. If her begging hadn't changed his mind, she would never change his mind. She would never, ever have him completely, and if she couldn't have him completely, then there was no point.

She took a step backward into the salon and quietly closed the door, pressing her lips together to try to keep herself from crying. But she couldn't.

He was the best thing that had ever happened to her, but it sometimes seemed that being with her actually tormented him.

# Chapter Eleven

Tanner arrived at his hotel exhausted from having spent the day looking at boats. In the course of twelve hours he'd discovered two things. First, he didn't know squat about boats or boating. Second, he got seasick. Really seasick. So seasick he knew he had to reconsider his choice of a new career.

Riding up in the elevator didn't help. In fact, nausea settled in his stomach like a rock, reminding him that everything in his life was out of sync. But then again, everything had been out of sync for a while. Since his divorce, nothing had been easy for him.

As the elevator door opened, he fished into his pocket for his key card. Because he was focused on that, he didn't notice that Emmalee Thorpe, his ex-wife, the last person on the face of the earth he ever wanted to see, was standing by his door, until he was right beside her.

"How did you get my room number?"

She smiled prettily. "I used an old Tanner McConnell trick. The one-hundred-dollar bill."

"Do you know that I could have the person who gave you that information fired?"

She shrugged. "You won't," she said, watching him open his hotel room door. "Because then you would have to be angry with your mother for giving me the name of your hotel. Can I come in?"

"Hell, no!" he said, glaring at her. The next time he saw his mother he would have to remind her to be more prudent with his whereabouts. "Haven't I suffered enough in one lifetime? Have you come here to tell me that I kicked your dog, too?"

Emma's expression became stricken and her eyes filled with tears.

"Oh, Emma," he groaned. Why was he always hurting her? "I'm sorry."

She sniffed. "Actually, that's what I came here to tell you. I'm sorry. I'm really, really, really sorry, Tanner," she said, then burst into uncontrollable tears.

"Oh, geez!" Tanner said, wrapping his arm around her shoulder then leading her into his hotel room. "Look, Emma, I didn't mean for any of this to happen." He guided her to the bed. "But you and I are oil and water or something. You just seem to bring out the worst in me."

As he said the last, she gave him a stricken look, then her sobs became louder, harder.

"Oh, for Pete's sake, Emma, don't!" he said, not quite sure what to do. "Look, I'm sorry. Can I get you a glass of water or something?"

She shook her head. "No. I'm okay. There are just some things I have to tell you, but you wouldn't talk to me in Wilmore..."

"Emma, we're divorced. You're remarried. You've

been remarried for nine of the ten years we've been divorced. There's nothing for us to talk about.''

She shook her head. ''No. We have lots of things to talk about. Really, really important things. Things that I should have told you sooner.'' Seeming in control now, she sniffed and grabbed a tissue from a box on the table by the bed. ''And the biggest thing is that when we got divorced I lied to you.''

''How?'' he asked suspiciously, not quite sure why it mattered after ten years, but suspecting this is how Emma coerced his whereabouts from his mother.

''I lied about why I wanted to get you out of my life.'' She paused and looked at him earnestly. ''But I only did it because I was desperate. Not only was I already seeing Artie Thorpe when you were out of town, but I was pregnant with his child.''

''What?'' Tanner asked stupefied. The information rolled over him like an ocean swell, and he had to sit. Since the nearest available space was the bed, he found himself seated by the woman he swore he would never get within two feet of again.

''I needed for you to leave. I needed to get a divorce, and Artie and I needed to get married because I was pregnant. But you kept saying you would try to work things out, and I didn't know what else to do. So I struck some low blows.''

''Some low blows?'' he said, looking at her incredulously. ''You told me I made you feel worthless. You told me I was so thoughtless, inconsiderate, and self-centered that you would rather *die* than be with me. I thought I was the scum of the earth.''

''I'm sorry.''

He gaped at her. ''Sorry? Emma, you told me I suffocated you, that I didn't know how to have a relationship, that I was mean-spirited and cruel.''

"I know.''

"All these years, I've tried to change and couldn't, because I didn't know how…. Was that because I didn't need to?''

Emma only looked at him. "Well, no. I wouldn't go that far. We had problems, Tanner. Big ones. But I was as much to blame as you.''

He put his head in his hands. "Why didn't you just tell me you were in love with Artie.''

"And have you go ballistic on Main Street and cause a horrible scandal?'' she said, then blew her nose. "I couldn't deal with that.''

"So you made me think I was a creep.''

"Tanner, you *were* self-centered, and you do have a tendency to tell people what to do, I only exaggerated the truth. And I did it to make it sound like there was no hope for *you* because I felt that was the only way I could prove there was no hope for *us*. Otherwise you would have just kept saying you wanted to work things out.'' She paused, caught his gaze and said, "I know what I did was wrong. I wanted to tell you I had blown everything out of proportion, but I just never got the chance.''

"What happened to your baby?''

"I had a miscarriage. Actually, that was the problem.'' She sighed heavily, then blew her nose again. "When I told Artie what I had said to you, he was very angry with me. But we also believed that once everybody realized I was pregnant and especially when the baby was born and people started counting months everybody—even you— would know that I had been pregnant when we divorced. You would recognize I had been unfaithful and you would understand that I'd made things sound worse than they were to get out of our marriage. But on our way to Las Vegas to get married, I had a miscarriage, and we changed our plans. Instead of getting married, we started dating. We waited a respectable year and then got married.''

"And you never bothered to correct the situation."

"I tried," Emma said. "Several times I wrote you letters, but I never had the guts to send them. I wanted to tell you in person. But more than that, you always seemed okay. Really okay, like you must not have believed me, or had gotten beyond it...then I saw you with Bailey. I heard the rumors, but I also saw you pulling away."

He sat in silence for several seconds then said, "A woman doesn't...isn't...well, unfaithful unless her husband drives her away."

"That's just the point, we were both at fault," Emma said, sounding tired and sad. "You were lost to me. Gone. Crazy with trying to figure out what to do with the rest of your life. But I was shallow and immature. Especially since you were going through a rough time." She drew a long breath and caught his gaze, her eyes pleading with him to understand. "But I've changed. I grew up. I'm very happily married now. And I want that for you."

"Why?"

"To be honest, so I can stop feeling guilty."

Tanner couldn't help it; he laughed. "I can't believe this."

"You have to believe it because it's the truth. It's also your problem right now. I think you gave up on love because we failed, and you shouldn't. Not only was I half to blame, but also," she said, smiling reluctantly, "don't you think that if I could change, you could change?"

He shrugged, ''I don't know.''

''Have you tried?''

''I don't know,'' he said again, confused and uncomfortable. Having the weight of guilt lifted from his shoulders was weird. True, he wasn't wholly exonerated, but he wasn't a complete creep, either. He was so accustomed to carrying the full burden for his divorce, he almost didn't know how to behave without it.

''If you think about it, Tanner, you can do anything you want. You always could.''

''Yes, I suppose I could,'' Tanner agreed, looking at Emma with different eyes. She wasn't a fragile porcelain doll he had hurt. She was a flesh-and-blood woman who, it turns out, had hurt him as much as he had hurt her. Ridiculous as it sounded, he could handle that. ''So, you're happy now?''

''Very.''

''And you want me to be happy now?''

''I *need* for you to be happy.''

Disoriented and confused, he ran his hand down his face. ''I feel like I'm starting all over again.''

''With a clean slate, Tanner. We were both wrong. But I was more wrong than you were,'' Emma said, then rose from the bed. ''And I feel 100 percent better now that I've told you.''

She said the last and walked to his hotel room door. She paused to say goodbye, and Tanner smiled and wished her well because there was no point not to, but his thoughts were in complete chaos. For the past ten years of his life he had pushed himself to be better than everybody professionally because he believed he couldn't have a personal, intimate relationship. After all, he had done his best with Emmalee and failed. Now he knew the failure wasn't his, but theirs, and he almost didn't know how to process the information. All he knew was that it overwhelmed him.

"I heard Tanner McConnell gets seasick!"

"No kidding," Cora Beth said as she snipped away at Mrs. Murphy's hair. Short and naturally curly, Mrs. Murphy's locks sprang back into place with every snip Cora took. "Who told you that?"

"His mother!"

"Well, I'll be."

Bailey tried not to listen as the conversation revolved around the one person in the entire world whom Bailey had ever loved. Her feelings for Tanner were so all encompassing that she didn't even think she had ever really loved Dennis. But Tanner wouldn't share the problem that haunted him, though she suspected it had something to do with his first marriage, and Bailey couldn't help him if he wouldn't talk with her. She couldn't help him. She couldn't have him. She boldly faced that knowledge every day of her life in the hope that one day the information would sink in and she could forget him. So far, no such luck.

Jimmy Farrah, son of the owners of Farrah Florists, pushed his way into the salon carrying a long white box. "Hey, Bailey, these are for you."

She walked over to her cash register, extracted a tip, and took the box from Jimmy.

"Ohh..." Cora cooed. "Flowers! Wonder who those are from?"

"Probably you," she said dully, because Cora had done everything in her power for the past two weeks to cheer her up. Though nothing had really worked, Bailey had gotten very good at pretending.

"I didn't send those," Cora said.

Both Cora and Mrs. Murphy stared expectantly at Bailey. Feeling oddly mean-spirited, Bailey said, "Yeah right. I'll bet you didn't."

Cora looked offended. "I didn't."

"Whatever," Bailey said, then started walking toward her office. "I think I'll open these in the back."

"Oh, Bailey!" Mrs. Murphy cried. "Come on, I deserve to see who sent those. I brought homemade cookies this morning."

"And for that I should thank you?" Bailey said with a laugh. "What I should do is make you and Ida Mae Ringler pay for a gym membership."

"You're never going to need a gym membership. You have one of those metabolisms that burns everything you take in."

Hearing the familiar voice, Bailey spun around. "Tanner?"

"Tanner!" Both Cora and Mrs. Murphy said in unison, both sounding as if they were swooning.

"You don't need a gym membership," Tanner said, walking into the salon. "But it was a good idea about going into the back to open the box."

"What's in here?" she said, eyeing him suspiciously.

"It's just a little something any normal man buys for the woman he's going to marry."

"Ohh!" Cora and Mrs. Murphy sounded as though they had gone into cardiac arrest.

Bailey's eyes narrowed. "I thought you couldn't change."

Tanner smiled. "Turns out I think I can."

"I could have told you that," Bailey began, but Tanner interrupted her.

"And I wouldn't have listened. Just like you're not

listening to me now about going to the back to open the box. So, we're sort of even."

"If I go to the back, does that mean you're going to explain all this to me?"

"In glorious detail."

"Okay," Bailey, said and started for her office.

Cora and Mrs. Murphy groaned.

"Just have a cookie, I'm sure I'll be out shortly," Bailey said because she had made up her mind, and there was nothing Tanner could say to make her change it. She had been hurt two times in her life, but Dennis stealing money was nothing compared to Tanner stealing her heart. She had two weeks' worth of getting over him under her belt, and he would have to go a long way to get her to give that up.

The minute the curtain closed behind them, Tanner grabbed her arms, spun her around and pulled her up for a long, open-mouthed kiss. Bailey's head reeled from it. The taste of him, the scent of him, the feeling of having his arms around her were so dear and familiar, she almost collapsed with joy.

"Oh, God, I love you," he said when he finally released her. "And I thought for sure you were going to be majorly mad at me."

"I was," she said, wondering where the hell her strength and conviction had gone. "I was majorly angry. I'm *still* angry."

"And you had every right to be because I never really explained things to you. But I have a good reason. I never understood them myself."

She stared at him. His handsome face, his beautiful eyes, the little spikes of yellow hair made even lighter from the time he had spent in Florida. "I heard you get seasick."

"I do. Terribly, terribly seasick. I don't want to move to Florida. It's a nice place to visit, but I'm afraid I'm not made to live there."

"And that's why you're here? Because you discovered you don't like Florida?"

He laughed. The sound rich and glorious. "No. I'm here because I love you and I desperately want to make a life with you. To have kids. Make a home...you know I can be a stay-at-home dad. I'm retired."

He said it with such a matter-of-fact tone that Bailey backed away from him. "Don't tease me."

"I'm not. I love you, Bailey," he said. "More than I've ever loved anybody or anything in my life. But I was afraid I would ruin the relationship like I ruined my marriage to Emma. But it turns out she was having an affair with Artie, so I hadn't ruined the relationship. We both had. But at least I had an excuse because of my knee." He paused, ran his hand across the back of his neck. "I'm rambling. It's kind of a complicated story..."

"She had an affair with Artie?"

"Yeah, someday I'll share the particulars, but right now I want you to open the box."

Bailey set the box on her desk and pulled on the big red bow. It gave easily, and she lifted the lid to discover a dozen long-stemmed roses. "This is the big mysterious thing you give to the woman you want to marry?" she asked curiously.

"Roses and the thing that's under them."

Bailey gave him a suspicious look. "Did you traumatize the Farrahs?" she asked, thinking he'd asked them to hide some filmy red teddy, or maybe edible underwear.

He laughed. "No, I packed the box. They only provided it...and the roses."

Bailey removed the delicate red flowers by lifting the tissue paper beneath them. When she saw the green-purple-and-orange print, she set the roses on the desk and picked up the garment. "Good God, it's a golf shirt...and it's horrible."

He smiled. "Isn't it?"

She stared at him. "*This* is what you think a man gives to the woman he wants to marry?"

"Yeah. It's symbolic," he said, looking at the golf shirt with love in his eyes. "First, it's want I want from you. Lots of common, ordinary days. Second, if I can think you're gorgeous and sexy in this, then I really, really must love you."

Tears unexpectedly sprang to Bailey's eyes. "Oh, Tanner, I must have loved you from the minute I met you, because I thought you looked really cute in your ugly golf shirt, too."

"Then it's official," he said, opening his arms to her. "We love each other enough that we should get married."

"Yeah, I think so," she agreed and stepped into his embrace. Warm, wonderful satisfaction rippled through her. But also another thought struck her. Her instincts had been right. No matter how much it hurt to watch him go, knowing he might not be back, he did have to figure this out for himself. And he had. But because he had, she knew he was hers forever. He wouldn't change his mind.

She pulled back so she could look at him. "I'm getting pretty good at this business of making the right move at the right time."

"Of course you are," he said, laughing lightly as he hugged her. "You're going to be great one day."

"Will you help me?"

"When I'm not watching kids."

She smiled. "We're going to have such a good time."

"Yes, we are."

"Should we show Mrs. Murphy and Cora the golf shirt?"

Tanner laughed. "Nah, let them think it's edible underwear."

* * * * *

**Don't miss the reprisal of
Silhouette Romance's popular miniseries**

**When
King Michael of
Edenbourg goes
missing,**

**his devoted
family and loyal
subjects make it
their mission to bring
him home safely!**

## Their search begins March 2001 and continues through June 2001.

On sale March 2001: **THE EXPECTANT PRINCESS**
by bestselling author **Stella Bagwell** (SR #1504)

On sale April 2001: **THE BLACKSHEEP PRINCE'S BRIDE**
by rising star **Martha Shields** (SR #1510)

On sale May 2001: **CODE NAME: PRINCE**
by popular author **Valerie Parv** (SR #1516)

On sale June 2001: **AN OFFICER AND A PRINCESS**
by award-winning author **Carla Cassidy** (SR #1522)

*Available at your favorite retail outlet.*

*Where love comes alive*™

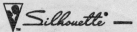
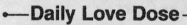

**SILHOUETTE® MAKES YOU A STAR!**

*Look in the back pages of all June Silhouette series books to find an exciting new contest with fabulous prizes! Available exclusively through Silhouette.*

*Don't miss it!*

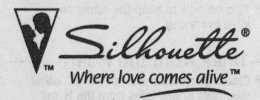

**Silhouette®**

*Where love comes alive™*

*P.S. Watch for details on how you can meet your favorite Silhouette author.*

Meet 50 loving dads in

# bobies
## & BACHELORS USA
## Take 4 FREE BOOKS,
## Plus get a FREE GIFT!

*Babies & Bachelors USA* is a heartwarming new collection of reissued novels featuring 50 sexy heroes from every state who experience the ups and downs of fatherhood and find time for love all the same. All of the books, hand-picked by our editors, are outstanding romances by some of the world's bestselling authors, including Stella Bagwell, Kristine Rolofson, Judith Arnold and Marie Ferrarella!

**Don't delay, order today! Call customer service at**
**1-800-873-8635.**
**Or**
**Clip this page and mail to The Reader Service:**

In U.S.A.
P.O. Box 9049
Buffalo, NY
14269-9049

In CANADA
P.O. Box 616
Fort Erie, Ontario
L2A 5X3

YES! Please send me four FREE BOOKS and FREE GIFT along with the next four novels on a 14-day free home preview. If I like the books and decide to keep them, I'll pay just $15.96* U.S. or $18.00* CAN., and there's no charge for shipping and handling. Otherwise, I'll keep the 4 FREE BOOKS and FREE GIFT and return the rest. If I decide to continue, I'll receive six books each month—two of which are always free—until I've received the entire collection. In other words, if I collect all 50 volumes, I will have paid for 32 and received 18 absolutely free!

267 HCK 4537
467 HCK 4538

| Name | (Please Print) | | |
|---|---|---|---|
| Address | | | Apt. # |
| City | | State/Prov. | Zip/Postal Code |

*Terms and prices subject to change without notice.
Sales Tax applicable in N.Y. Canadian residents will be charged applicable provincial taxes and GST. All orders are subject to approval.

DIRBAB02

© 2000 Harlequin Enterprises Limited

# COMING NEXT MONTH

**#1522 AN OFFICER AND A PRINCESS—Carla Cassidy**
*Royally Wed: The Stanburys*
Military law forbade their relationship, but couldn't stop the feelings Adam Sinclair and Princess Isabel Stanbury secretly harbored. Could they rescue the king, uncover the conspirators—*and* find the happily-ever-after they yearned for?

**#1523 HER TYCOON BOSS—Karen Rose Smith**
*25th Book*
Mac Nightwalker was wary of gold-digging women, but struggling single mom Dina Corcoran's money woes touched the cynical tycoon. He offered her a housekeeping job, and Dina quickly turned Mac's house into the home he'd never had. Did the brooding bachelor dare let his Cinderella slip away?

**#1524 A CHILD FOR CADE—Patricia Thayer**
*The Texas Brotherhood*
Years earlier, Abby Garson had followed her father's wishes and married another, although her heart belonged to Cade Randell. Now Cade was back in Texas. But Abby had been keeping a *big* secret about the little boy Cade was becoming very attached to....

**#1525 THE BABY SEASON—Alice Sharpe**
*An Older Man*
Babies, babies everywhere! A population explosion at Jack Wheeler's ranch didn't thrill producer Roxanne Salyer—she didn't think she was mommy material. But Jack's little girl didn't find anything lacking in Roxanne's charms, and neither did the divorced doctor daddy....

**#1526 BLIND-DATE BRIDE—Myrna Mackenzie**
Tired of fielding the prospective husbands her matchmaking brothers tossed her way, Lilah Austin asked Tyler Westlake to be her pretend beau. Then Tyler realized that he didn't want anyone to claim Lilah but him! What was a determined bachelor to do...?

**#1527 THE LITTLEST WRANGLER—Belinda Barnes**
They'd shared a night of passion—and a son James Scott knew nothing about. Until Kelly Matthews showed up with a toddler—the spitting image of his daddy! When the time came for Kelly to return to college, could James convince her he wanted both of them to stay...forever?

RSCNM0501